HI!!

STAY "HAIR BRAINED..."

THE

FIFTEENTH

OF JUNE

[signature]

Brent Jones

OCT 28 2017

The Fifteenth of June

Copyright © 2017 Brent Jones

Visit the author's website at AuthorBrentJones.com.

Edited by Laura Mae Isaacman (Clyde Editing).

Cover design by Victoria Cooper.

ISBN-13: 978-1543276848

ISBN-10: 1543276849

*To Andréa . . . for believing
in me no matter what I do next.*

Chapter 1

The Stone Goblin was unusually busy for a Friday night. It was the sort of place where pretentious twentysomethings gathered after work, though no one knew why. The music was loud, the air was stale, and the drinks were overpriced.

Still, this bar had come to feel like home for Drew. He stood at a high top table with Neil, a former colleague and his closest friend. They had a tab running at the bar but had lost count hours before. Drew swayed, unsteady on his feet, looking into his empty glass, silently praying for a refill of whiskey.

Neil had just finished his latest vodka soda. He narrowed his eyes and scanned The Stone Goblin in search of his next conquest.

An attractive server with bronze skin, who looked to be college age, made her way through the crowd and stopped at their table. She had on a short kilt and a low cut top that displayed generous cleavage. Her face shone with naivety and her voice carried over the music. "Ready for another round, gentlemen?"

Neil looked at Drew's empty glass. "I know you do."

Drew looked up. "Yeah, I do."

Neil peered at Drew for a moment, displeased by his lack of enthusiasm. He placed a hand on the server's lower back. He pulled her close and spoke softly. "What's your name?"

"Becca," she replied.

"Becca," Neil echoed. He paused for effect, casting a furtive glance in Drew's direction. "Becca," he repeated, extending his other hand. "I'm Neil."

Becca shook Neil's hand. Her breasts jiggled.

Without releasing his grip, Neil nodded his head toward Drew. "This is my friend, Drew."

She looked at Drew, his messy hair, unkempt stubble, and the slight gut that hung over his pants. He was visibly underdressed, even for The Stone Goblin. Not that he tried to repel women—it came to him naturally. Becca gave him a timid smile, then quickly returned her focus to Neil. He was good-looking, tall, with dark features and expensive tastes. His clothes were trendy and fitted, every hair on his head styled with purpose.

"My friend here just lost his job, so I'm cheering him up." Neil slid his hand down to Becca's ass. "So we're going to need something a bit more interesting."

Becca stifled a giggle, gently removing his hand from her kilt. She seemed uncomfortable and flattered all at once. "What should I bring you?"

Neil looked her up and down. "Your choice. But bring three."

"Are you expecting someone?"

"You."

"I can't drink on the job," she playfully protested.

"What time are you off?" Neil made no effort to disguise his attention on her chest.

Becca blushed and vanished back into the sea of bodies.

"Fuck, what I'd do to her," Neil mused.

"What's special about her?"

"She's practically begging for it."

Are women attracted to his cockiness, or is he cocky because women throw themselves at him? Drew could be articulate when needed, but preferred the company of his own thoughts. He was all but physically absent in most social situations, lost in his own head. His disinterest in conversing with the outside world seemed to underscore Neil's social prowess. "I've got news," he said, changing the subject.

"You've got good news, bro. You ditched the bitch. You're a free man now."

Drew had broken up with his girlfriend just a month earlier. He and Heather had been together five years and she was, in her own way, imperfect. She was personable and stable, educated and thoughtful—all qualities that made Drew uncomfortable.

"Not what I meant," Drew slurred. "Found a new place to live."

"That was fast."

"Yeah, well, sleeping on your couch motivated me."

"Hey, it's a nice couch. Cost me a lot of money."

Becca reappeared with two shot glasses filled with a clear liquid. "Here you are, boys." She placed both glasses in front of Neil, who slid one over to Drew.

"What's this?" Drew asked.

"It's alcohol," Neil replied. "Just drink it."

As Becca turned to walk away, Neil grabbed her arm. She turned around, locking her eyes with his. "You never told me what time you get off."

Becca smiled and leaned in, pressing her body against him. "If you're still here, I'll find you." She wandered away.

Neil looked pleased. "Told you she'd fuck."

"Congrats. Anything with tits and a heartbeat, huh?"

"Anything with *big* tits," he said with a laugh. "It's an important distinction."

They threw back their shots. They wobbled in silence,

disinterested in their surroundings—music, laughter, the clink of glasses, and obnoxious conversations.

Neil was first to reengage. "So you got a place?"

"Yeah. Nothing special, but it's mine. Good place to hide out since me and Heather split."

"Why are you hiding out, bro? You're what? Twenty-seven? Twenty-eight?"

"Twenty-eight."

"Twenty-eight," Neil repeated. "You're in the prime of your life. You should be out banging sluts, not hiding alone at home."

"Sometimes I like to be alone."

Neil wrinkled his face in disgust. "I've known you, what? Two years? Three now?"

"Three."

"Three fucking years we've worked together. And I've never seen you too scared to talk to new people."

Drew gave his booze-soaked brain a moment to process Neil's remark. "I'm not scared. I just don't like it."

Drew first met Neil working outside sales for an office supplies firm, The Ascension Group. Neil excelled at closing the deal because he could be charming. He was excellent at reading people and telling them what they wanted to hear.

Drew, on the other hand, excelled for different reasons. After high school, he decided against college, and his lack of formal education left him with few career paths to follow. He worked odd jobs to get by until an online job ad tempted him to apply for a sales gig. As fate would have it, the hiring manager gave Drew a chance—his first and only salaried position and in a field he couldn't have been less excited for. It turned out that his indifference toward people, the very social disorders that had burdened him since childhood, propelled him toward success. His lack of empathy allowed him to be persistent to a fault, fearless to call on new prospects.

Selling had its drawbacks, too, of course—the entire process was exhausting for Drew. Most human interactions were. He found himself mentally withdrawn, progressively so, both at home and on the job. Alcohol had become his one true companion, a daily love affair he had learned to prioritize long before his career in sales began. Drew drank to escape the isolation that his drinking fortified, an irony that Heather had never been able to accept.

But it wasn't until recent months that Drew began experimenting with drugs. Weed at first, which he handled with ease, then cocaine and the occasional pill. The effects were almost immediate, especially at work. He had arrived an hour late to a client meeting earlier that week, visibly high, and butchered the deal. He got fired the same day.

"Still can't believe you let her keep your place, bro," Neil said, changing the subject. "That's like rule number one of living with a broad. You move her into your place so when shit goes tits up, you can kick her the fuck out."

"Yeah, well, Heather loved our apartment. And it didn't matter to me."

Becca bounced her way back to the table with the fervor of a cheerleader. She set down three shot glasses and grinned at Neil. "I'm off now," she teased.

"Should we call it a night?" Drew asked, leaning forward on the table.

It took Neil a second to acknowledge what Drew had said. He raised his index finger to Becca. "Can we have a sec?"

She rolled her eyes, feigning annoyance, then downed one of the shots. "Sure. I'll be outside." She pranced out of sight.

"Bro, it's great that you found a place. I'll come check it

out sometime."

"All right."

"But listen to me. Fuck Hillary—"

"Heather."

"Heather, whatever," Neil said. "There's plenty more broads out there for you." But he didn't look convinced.

"I think women prefer guys with jobs."

Neil laughed. "Yeah, you're probably right. You looking?"

"I, uh, haven't found anything with the prestige of selling paperclips and toner just yet."

"Always a joker." Neil grabbed his car keys off the table. "Trust me, bro. You're the lucky one. I'm still stuck at that shithole. Thinking of getting out soon myself." He tossed back one of the remaining shots. "Want me to drop off your stuff tomorrow?"

Drew downed the final shot, a thin smile on his face. "Nah. I've got more good news for you."

"What's that?"

"I already moved out today while you were at work. Means you can fuck her on your nice couch now, if you want."

Neil winked on his way out, but Drew lingered for a moment, aware of his environment for the first time in hours. He found himself besieged by an army of drunks—the types of people who actually enjoy the company of other drunks. *God, look at them. Some of them actually look like they're having fun.* He took in the sights, the sounds, and the smells of intoxication—fleeting sensory evidence of a night he was likely to forget—then staggered out to the parking lot. Neil's Mercedes was already gone.

Drew climbed into his aged hatchback and started the engine. The dashboard told him it was two o'clock in the morning.

He caught his own lifeless reflection in the rearview mirror—dead, bloodshot eyes and a head that gently bobbed in circles. He shut off the engine, pulled out his cell phone, and painstakingly figured out how to place a call. After three rings, an older man answered.

"Dad, it's Drew. You still up?"

Chapter 2

Drew opened his eyes to rays of morning sunshine accentuated through clouds of thick smoke. He was on an old couch, fully dressed, arms folded, trying to remember how he got there. It wasn't that Drew avoided driving drunk out of principle. He just needed assurance that not everything in his life was changing at once, and the house he grew up in served as nothing if not a monument to days gone by.

The room reeked of stale smoke. He sat up and surveyed a living space that hadn't changed in decades. Worn drapes, peeling wallpaper, and an old-style television with a miniature screen. The entire house was decorated with age and nicotine stains.

His father sat nearby at a card table watching the news with the volume down low. He stubbed out a cigarette in an overflowing ashtray and lit another.

"Love what you've done with the place," Drew said, his mouth dry.

Russell smirked without taking his eyes off the television. "Morning, smartass."

Nearly twenty years had passed since Drew's mother had died. Angela had left behind two young boys—Drew and Logan. Before Russell became a widower, he had been passionate, energetic, even optimistic at times. But nothing was the same after. He was now obese with a long white beard,

steely eyes, and yellow fingers. His face was worn well beyond his fifty-six years. Aside from bowling on Monday
nights and working odd jobs, Russell was a complete shut-
in. He also had a tendency to watch television in his underwear, and this morning was no exception.

"Thanks for coming to get me," Drew said.

"Looks like you had fun."

"Not as much fun as Neil had."

Drew knew that his father never cared much for Neil.
Russell considered Neil a bit arrogant for his tastes. A man
secure in himself didn't need an expensive car, tailored
clothes, or even a steady paycheck, for that matter.

Drew envied Neil's confidence and charisma at times—he
was likable on the exterior and people kissed his ass everywhere he went. Drew tragically found himself with the opposite problem—good intentioned, but unpalatable to most
whose paths he crossed.

But the envy he felt extended only to a point. Neil lived a
conspicuous lifestyle, while Drew preferred privacy and solitude, to live incognito. But chasing vicarious thrills through
Neil offered him just the right amount of escapism.

Russell coughed into a cloth napkin then folded it neatly
on the card table. He took a drag off his cigarette. "How's
work going?"

Drew hesitated. "I, uh, got laid off this week."

"They lay off Neil, too?"

"Uh, no. Neil still works there. He made the cut."

"See, you've got to understand, son. There's two types of
guys in this world. There's guys like you and me, and there's
guys like Neil."

"Winners and losers?"

"Something like that. Guys who think they're in control,
and guys like us who live in the moment. Who accept life as

it is."

"What kind of guy does that make my brother?"

His father thought for a moment, extinguishing one cigarette and lighting another. "I'm still trying to figure that one out. And so is he."

It was no secret that Drew and his father were close. But Russell's relationship with Logan was complicated. Logan had always been a serious kid, despite being two years younger than Drew, and he had never seen eye-to-eye with his father.

Logan left home as a teenager in hopes of a fresh start. Or as Drew described it, an opportunity for Logan to turn his back on their father. Russell and Logan now only saw each other once a year—every fifteenth of June, the anniversary of Angela's death.

After leaving home, Logan finished high school and pursued higher education. He became the first Thomson to graduate from college, eventually going on to law school and becoming a junior associate for a criminal defense firm in town.

"What about you? You working right now?" Drew asked.

Russell cleared his throat. "Yeah, here and there. Got a gig working for this scrappy little Jew on the east side. Night shift. Cleaning printing presses."

"Sounds glamorous." Drew snickered.

"S'pose you got a better job lined up?"

"Maybe. Thinking of retiring."

Russell laughed until he choked, his broken lungs heaving and screaming for respite. His face contorted in anguish. He hacked into his napkin and took another puff.

Drew got off the couch and walked over to the card table. He picked up the pack of cigarettes and mimed a look of horror. "Dad, look here," he said, pointing to the warning label. "Says here these things will fucking kill you." He solemnly tossed the pack back on the table and returned to the couch.

"If your mother were alive, she wouldn't want to hear you talking like that."

"If mom were alive, she'd tell you to go get that cough checked out."

His father's eyes were planted on his ashtray. "S'pose you're right."

"But at the rate you're going, you might see mom soon enough."

Russell spluttered into his napkin again. He stomped out his smoke and lit another.

"What time is it?" Drew asked.

Russell turned his head to a grandfather clock in the adjoining room. "Time for breakfast. Bacon and eggs good with you?"

"Yeah, good with me. Good for your cholesterol, too."

"Yeah, s'pose my doctor would tell me to eat oats or something, right?"

* * *

Drew sat with his father—who had put on pants for breakfast—at the same end of a hardwood table, its length almost the full measure of the dining room. Periodicals from years gone by, a wilted plant, and other relics occupied its remaining surface area. Atop the clutter sat a framed photo of Angela, taken on her thirtieth birthday. She had soft features, fair skin, and wore elegant diamond earrings.

"How's Heather?" Russell asked, taking a small slurp of his coffee.

Drew knew that his father had always been fond of Heather. She was a plain girl of average height, slim build, straight hair, freckles, and a bit conservative. A girl, his father often asserted, not so different in character from his mother—devoted and nurturing by nature.

"Dad, me and Heather broke up like a month ago. I told you."

Russell was cutting his food into small forkfuls—easier to chew without triggering a coughing fit. "Yeah, s'pose you did." He paused to chew a mouthful of bacon. "Thought maybe you changed your mind."

"We wanted different things. So I ended it."

"Sure. She want a baby or something?"

"I guess so. But not right away."

"She sleep with someone else?"

"No, Dad. That's not it."

"Did you?"

"No."

"Then what?"

I need a drink. That's what. Jesus fuck. Drew sighed. It was unlike his father to push but he knew why. In three days, they would observe the twentieth anniversary of his mother's death. A time of year that always seemed to leave Russell searching for answers.

Angela looked vibrant this morning, lively even. Drew noticed his father taking a sudden interest in her presence at the table, as though she had caught him off guard.

Russell picked up her frame. "Man was not meant to walk through life alone, son," he said. He popped a cigarette in his mouth and fumbled for his lighter. "Angie knew that."

Drew swallowed his last bite of breakfast while Russell peered at the frame. He sucked on his smoke, inhaling deeply, predictably followed by coughing and choking.

"Dad," Drew began. But no other words came.

His father appeared content to bask in nostalgia for a moment, using his fork to play with his unfinished breakfast.

"It is what it is," he finally said, returning Angela to her original spot. "But it wasn't always this way, son."

Drew stood up, cleared the table, and walked to the kitchen sink to start the dishes. His father's despair was palpable, and Drew found himself emotionally unequipped and stone sober—a combination that left him unsettled under the best of circumstances.

He was eight when his mother had passed away. Drew recalled the rainy June evening she went missing. His father knew something was wrong when she hadn't returned home after running an errand. He contacted the police, but it wasn't until the early hours of the next morning that the call came in—Angela Thomson's body was found in Northwood Park.

The details of her rape and bludgeoning followed days later. Russell tried in vain to shield his boys from the gruesome details. In so doing, it seemed he avoided confronting his own loss, never fully accepting her fate.

At the time, Drew was too young to understand yet too old to ever forget. He was repeatedly tested throughout childhood for dissociative disorders. His teachers worried about his antisocial behavior. They couldn't conceive of a traumatized young boy struggling to socialize and adapt.

Logan, on the other hand, as the youngest, seemed mostly unaffected. The gory particulars of Angela's death had eluded him. Police at the house, his mother's face on the news, candlelight vigils, and never-ending theories crafted by creative journalists: Was it an affair gone sideways, or perhaps a robbery turned violent? Could it have been a matter of wrong place and wrong time? These were questions the Thomson family never got answered. A brutal crime without reason. A family without closure.

Angela Thomson, born Angela Nowak, was survived by

her mother and sister. Both of whom blamed Russell for her death—as though he should have been able to prevent it. Without living relatives and shut out by the Nowaks, Russell raised Drew and Logan on his own.

He sold his commercial trucking business for pennies on the dollar shortly thereafter. He sold their house, too, moving his sons across town. It was a desperate attempt at distancing his boys from tragedy—desperate and unsuccessful. Over the next two decades, Russell became a prisoner of that very house.

"Drew?" Russell had slipped into the kitchen undetected, despite his labored movements and heavy wheezing.

He was startled. "Yeah?"

"It was good to see you."

Drew felt his phone vibrate in his pocket. He pulled it out with wet hands and saw a text message from Logan. "Just finished the dishes, so I'm gonna get going," he said.

"All right." Russell refilled his coffee, lit a fresh cigarette, and followed Drew to the door. "You heard from your brother lately?"

"No. Not in a while now."

"I figured as much."

Drew nodded and walked out.

Chapter 3

Drew took a cab back to The Stone Goblin. Russell would likely have given him a lift, but Drew didn't want to trouble his father to leave the house twice in so many hours. He walked over to his car at the far end of the lot. Bald tires, a cracked windshield, and a faded bumper sticker that read, Watch Out for The Idiot Behind Me. It was just as he had left it. Drew climbed in the driver's seat, reached for the glove box, and pulled out a joint. He sparked it up, rolled down the window, and watched time pass.

The weekend lunch crowd filed in and out of The Stone Goblin. Friends swapped greetings near the entrance. A young man walked an elderly woman—presumably his grandmother—across the parking lot. A couple guys left with takeout containers. A server took a smoke break a few feet from the front door. A pigeon defecated from the roof. Minutes passed and Drew felt his tension subside. His troubles went up in smoke and the world became tolerable again. He glanced down at the text message from his brother.

Logan: *Call me*

Brevity was a trait Drew admired. But Logan was nothing if not aggravating and Drew knew better than to call him without first clearing his head. He kept in touch with Logan mostly out of obligation. His brother was, after all, one of his only living relatives. Every couple of months they would have lunch together—usually on a weekday. It always ended with Drew remembering that his brother had a personality like sandpaper.

The joint burned down to its paper filter, Drew took in one final puff and threw the crutch out of his car window. He started the engine and took off. With his free hand, he dialed Logan from his short list of contacts.

"Hello?" Logan answered.

"Hey," Drew said.

"Hi, Andrew. How are you?" Logan always spoke in a formal way that Drew found unsettling.

"Yeah, I'm good. I'm just leaving Dad's."

"How's Russell doing these days?"

Russell? You mean Dad, dickhead. "Oh, he's just like me—high on life, if you can believe it."

"Yeah?"

"Surprised you haven't found time to see him, to be honest." Drew stopped at a red light. Fines were steep for holding a cell phone while driving, but he was certain no one was watching.

"I'll see him in a few days," Logan said. "I've just been so busy."

"Busy defending killers, huh?"

"I'm a junior associate, Andrew. I'm not defending anyone just yet."

Drew had once read that people respond to grief differently. Some shut down. Some become anxious and talkative. And some grow up to ensure predators get a fair trial.

Logan spoke again. "How's work?"

"Good. Yeah, really good. Thanks for asking. I, uh, think they're gonna give me a promotion pretty soon."

"A promotion?" Logan sounded more surprised than impressed.

"Yeah, for sure. I've put in three years now. They owe it to me."

"Well," Logan said at last, "I'll stop by your office one day soon. We'll do lunch again."

Yeah, you do that.

"What's the game plan for Tuesday?" Logan asked.

The game plan? What a class act you are. "Well, if all goes to plan, we'll have a beautiful family reunion."

"Very funny."

"We're gonna do the same shit as every year, Logan. We're going to meet at Hillcrest at eleven o'clock, drop off some flowers, talk to Mom's corpse for a while, and head home."

Logan paused. "Eleven, you said?"

"Yes, Logan. Eleven."

"I'm going to have to move a meeting."

"Sorry to trouble you."

Drew arrived at his apartment complex. The superintendent had given him a clicker for the underground parking, but it wasn't working, so he pulled into a spot for visitors.

"Is that all, Logan?"

"What do you mean?"

"Is that all you wanted? To make sure you knew the time?"

"Oh—" Logan broke off for a moment, "Well, I wanted to hear how you're doing, too."

"I'm just great. Don't worry about me."

"Did you find a new place to live yet?"

Drew climbed out of his car and eyed the immense and decrepit structure he now called home. "I did. And it's nice." He wasn't sure he'd ever get used to the smell of dumpsters in the parking lot. "Gotta say, I'm happier than I've ever been."

"That's good, Andrew. You've got to do what makes you happy in life."

Drew slammed his car door. "I've got to run. I'll see you Tuesday."

Chapter 4

Drew had picked up the keys to his apartment a few days earlier, having taken possession partway through the month—but he had only moved in mere hours before joining Neil at The Stone Goblin the night before. He felt an odd sense of enthusiasm to be home.

The apartment door opened into a small and vacant living space. A beat up mountain bike leaned against the wall, a laptop on a stack of boxes, a mattress on the floor, a cheaply constructed rocking chair with faded padding in the corner, and—Heather. She was sitting in the rocking chair reading something on her phone. She looked up at Drew as he entered.

"Jesus," he exclaimed. "You ever heard of calling?"

"Sorry. I just got here and the door was unlocked." Heather got to her feet. "I brought you food."

"Why?"

"I thought you might be hungry."

Drew walked over to his assortment of boxes. He rummaged through one box, and then another. He triumphantly removed a bottle with a bit of whiskey left. "You shouldn't have," he replied.

Heather made her way into the cramped kitchen. It featured dated appliances, walls speckled with grease stains, chipped floor tiles, and counters full of burn marks. She picked up a Chinese takeout container and presented it to Drew through a small pass-through connecting the two rooms.

"No, really," he said. "You shouldn't have. I just had breakfast with Dad."

She set the container on the kitchen counter. "How have you been?"

Drew opened the whiskey bottle and took a swig. It burned beautifully. "Okay, I guess."

"You like it here?" Heather was attempting to be polite. There was nothing to like about the apartment aside from a toilet that flushed and shut windows that kept out the stench of garbage below.

"Yeah, I like it fine," he replied, taking another swig and setting the bottle down on a box. Drew walked into the kitchen, the tight space forcing him to brush against her. He opened his fridge, observing its chilled interior for the first time, and tossed the takeout container in. "Why are you really here?" he asked, turning around to face her.

"I miss you," she said with a slight tremble.

Drew brushed past her again, grabbing the whiskey bottle and taking another swig.

A fat tear spilled down Heather's cheek. Then another.

Oh fuck, don't do this.

When Drew ended their relationship a month earlier, he had taken Heather out for dinner. Tacos—nothing fancy— but he had hoped that a public venue would prevent an outburst. It hadn't. Between bites, Drew recited his reasons for breaking things off. But his rehearsed statements and cool disinterest had the opposite effect, resulting in a public spectacle worthy of primetime television. Heather had felt blindsided—equal parts hurt, humiliated, and confused.

The dust settled once Drew had packed his things and

sought refuge with Neil. But even now, Heather seemed intent on reconciliation.

"I moved out a month ago, Heather. What's there to miss?"

"Lots."

Drew rolled his eyes.

"I miss your jokes. You always could make me laugh. And I miss us talking. Like you were always the first person I wanted to talk to about my day, and now I can't do that."

Drew stood, frozen. He lacked empathy, but he wasn't emotionless. Not a monster, just unsure how to react. He liked Heather, and he didn't take pleasure in her agony, but her vulnerability petrified him. Each tear made him want to leap from his tenth floor balcony.

His thoughts turned to romantic comedies he had seen— Heather never could get enough of them. Hollywood liked to choose handsome, dashing, and passionate men for lead roles. Knights in shining armor and firemen types, mostly. Men who could meet a woman, win her heart, get in her pants, and live happily ever after in under two hours. Men who were nothing like Drew. Then again, life wasn't a movie. But after five years, Drew found himself unable to reciprocate Heather's passion. She loved him to a fault, often overwhelming him with affection. The more Heather cared for him, the less deserving he felt. And the more he retreated inward, the more of herself Heather gave. The guilt had become overwhelming—he knew she deserved better, but also knew she would never readily let him go. So Drew firmly resolved to shut her out. She would find a way to move on eventually.

"I'm sorry," Drew said, returning to the moment. He owed her more than a simple apology but decided it was a good place to start. "I just don't know what to say. " He took several more swallows of whiskey.

Heather and Drew had spent most of their twenties together, having first met when she was in her final year of college. She graduated with a degree in biology and had immediately started working as a research assistant at the metropolitan zoo. They moved in together shortly thereafter.

Where she was disciplined and ambitious, Drew was mostly unfocused and subdued. Heather had come to terms with their differences, often describing herself as the gas and Drew as the brake—a perfect match, in a sense. It was clear that he avoided his feelings and feared change, but that had never been enough to deter her.

She sniffled. "This was a mistake."

Drew felt a pang of remorse as Heather turned toward the door. "No," he said at last. "Stay."

She turned around.

"Uh, please." He pulled the cheap rocking chair out from the corner. "Sit."

Heather gave him a lopsided grin despite her wet face and red eyes. "Where will you sit, silly?"

He pretended to frantically look about. "How about right here?" he finally asked, parking himself on the floor.

Heather slowly eased herself onto the chair. "That works." Her eyes darted from one corner of the apartment to the other. "So," she asked, "why Palmer Heights? Didn't know you liked this part of town."

"Felt right."

"You could have kept the apartment, babe."

Don't call me babe.

"It's as much yours as it is mine," she continued.

"I know, but you always liked it there."

"I liked it there because you were there."

"Well, it's yours now."

"It could still be ours, Drew."

Drew tipped back the whiskey, finishing the bottle. He tossed its empty glass shell on the floor next to his mattress.

Heather eyed the empty bottle. "Have you been drinking every day?"

"Only on special occasions, I swear."

"Like this one?"

Most definitely like this one.

She peered down at him from the rocking chair, an unsettled look on her face. "Have you been gambling again, too?"

Drew had struggled with gambling—particularly the online variety—for years.

"It's not gambling if you always win."

"If you always win," she repeated. "Drew, I paid your half of the bills for years while you blew every dime you made." Her expression hardened. "You know what? Never mind. It's not my problem anymore."

Heather had a tight circle of friends she had first met in college. A group of gossipy and affluent young women—the Indiscreet Elite, as Drew described them—who chewed through men like kale and pumpkin spice. They had tried more than once to convince Heather that she could do better. Their attempts to persuade her were thinly veiled, often resulting in crass remarks about Drew while he was present. But the more they pressed, the more Heather pushed back, waiting for his best self to emerge. A version of himself that Drew wasn't sure existed.

"I lied for you. For years, Drew." She sighed. "I covered your ass. I kept you fed and clothed."

"I'm not a charity case, Heather. Quit patting yourself on the back. It wasn't that bad."

"You know what? Fuck you." She rose from the chair and

strode to the door.

"Heather, wait." Drew stood, unsteady on his feet.

"What, Drew? What?"

"Look, I know I'm not perfect . . . "

"No kidding."

"Heather, I—I want you to be happy."

She listened but her eyes betrayed her disbelief.

"That's why I left," he said softly, "so you could be happy. You—you can finally be happy without me."

Heather wiped away fresh tears then approached him, defenseless. "But I'm not happy," she remarked. "Are you?"

"No." Drew was being honest.

Heather cautiously extended her hand, brushing her fingers against his cheek. "Then why don't you come home?"

He searched for a reasonable explanation but couldn't find one, opting instead to stare at the parquet floor. "I don't know."

"Do you still love me?"

No. He raised his head. "Yes."

A flicker of hope flashed across her face.

"But I've made my choice." He paused. "I'm sorry."

"I'll go," she managed with a slight nod. The door shut slowly behind her.

Drew fell back on his mattress, thankful for the familiar silence.

* * *

Several hours passed and Drew awoke to darkness. He slowly got to his feet and turned on the kitchen light. In the absence of a lamp, it would do. He pulled the cold Chinese food from the refrigerator—pork and pineapple fried rice—and relocated to the balcony. Using his thumb and forefinger, he shoveled bits into his mouth. Ethnic cuisines wafted into his nostrils from adjoining units, pairing offensively with the scent of trash below. Drew felt no less invigorated to consume his dinner. He leaned over the railing. Miniature people scurried between high-rise units, corner stores, transit stops, and fast food joints. Horns and sirens blared in the distance. An old bum pushed a shopping cart through a nearby parking lot. It was Saturday night and the people of Palmer Heights were alive.

A starry night sky blanketed the distant skyline. Palmer Heights was within city limits, but it was a neighborhood that most—especially young professionals—seldom ventured to. To move here was social suicide. What the Indiscreet Elite called "settling." But Drew didn't care. It was home now. It was where he was supposed to be.

Drew finished his food, tossed the container off the balcony, and returned indoors. He slid a large cardboard box in front of his rocking chair and took a seat. The flaps of the box were opened, revealing a treasure trove of books, charging cables, playing cards, glass pipes, and a single framed photo of Heather. He gripped the frame, shut his eyes, and then dropped it on the floor.

Drew closed the flaps, placed his laptop on its surface, lifted its screen upright, and clicked a familiar icon on his desktop. A small light illuminated next to his webcam. His face—complete with scruff, chapped lips, and dark circles—appeared on the screen. He took a deep breath and clicked the red record button at the bottom of the application.

"Hi," he began. Drew caught his crooked posture in the video preview and adjusted himself on the chair. "It's been a little while now, I guess. A few days at least, right? Well, I'm—I'm going to keep this one short. I need to go pick up a bottle of something and, uh, the store closes in an hour or so." Drew glanced at the on-screen timer. Twenty-six seconds of his life digitally captured. "So," he continued,

"Heather just left. I, uh, I hope I'm not making a mistake." Thirty-four seconds. "I wish sometimes I could see myself the way she sees me. It's like no matter how bad I fuck up, she never gives up on me. But I feel . . . nothing for her. Just emptiness. I'm ready to leave her in the past."

After his mother died, Drew was taken to see a number of counselors. Sadness Doctors, he had dubbed them. They were supposed to make his sadness go away. But it seemed to Drew, even then, that the Sadness Doctors were more interested in getting money out of his father than helping him.

Except for the last one, who Drew encountered just shy of this tenth birthday. A heavyset woman with curly hair, a slight accent, and crooked teeth. Her breath smelled like coffee. She didn't smile much. But Drew had clung to her every word. To this day, he couldn't recall her name. He simply remembered her as Coffee Breath. In their first session together, she had encouraged Drew to keep a diary. Somewhere he could write down his thoughts. "You need to live your truth," Coffee Breath had told him, "and the more honest you can be with yourself, the more alive you'll start to feel."

Drew never really grasped what that meant—living his truth—even as an adult. But in that first session, she handed Drew a lined notebook and a pencil. He sat staring at a blank page, unsure of what to write. "Describe whatever comes to mind," she had coaxed.

He ended up writing a short story about meeting a bear in the woods. The bear seemed scary at first, but it turned out he wasn't so bad. The bear even shared a bit of his honey with Drew before returning to his cave. He never saw the bear again. The moral of the story, in his young mind, was to avoid getting too close to anyone. Sooner or later, people would leave his side, taking their honey with them.

He had tried to share his writing with Coffee Breath, just as he was accustomed to showing his schoolwork to teachers, but she refused to look at it. "These are your special moments, Andrew," she had explained. "And no one else gets to experience them—no one but you."

"Then why write them down?" he had asked.

"Because it's only when you become aware of yourself—your thoughts, your choices, and your feelings—that you can begin to take ownership of your life." She had spoken softly and slowly to Drew, as adults do when reasoning with a child. "Your life is made up of small and special moments. And when you learn to capture those special moments, both the good ones and the bad ones, you begin to live with purpose. Otherwise, your life will just be a series of passing seconds and minutes. Do you understand?"

"Yes." But he hadn't understood a word of it.

"Good. Don't let anyone steal your special moments, Andrew. No one can take them from you."

At the end of the session, Russell returned with Logan in tow. When he had asked Coffee Breath how it went, she mentioned the diary. Russell picked up the lined notebook despite Coffee Breath objecting. He read Drew's entry about the friendly bear and anger rushed across his face. He tore the book in half and tossed it in the trash can. "Bullshit," he had called it. "I'm paying you this kind of money to write fairy tales with my son? What the hell is wrong with you? Why aren't you fucking quacks fixing him?"

That was the last Sadness Doctor Drew ever saw.

Eighteen years later, Drew still kept a diary—and no one knew. Not his father, not Neil or his brother, not even Heather. He kept his thoughts private, just as Coffee Breath had taught him to. As a kid, he wrote on scrap pieces of paper, as a teenager it was hardcover journals and cassette tapes, and as an adult, it was videos on his computer. Hundreds of video files now spanned his collection, arranged in reverse chronological order, dating back for years. Some of them were as short as two minutes. Others carried on for an hour. It depended how much private time Drew could muster—and how much had happened since his last recording.

Two minutes and forty-three seconds had elapsed in the video. Drew returned to reality and looked straight into the camera—as if to make eye contact with his digital self—then continued.

"The thing is, I'm an asshole. And I know it. I—I don't mean to be." He shut his eyes, allowing himself a moment to collect his thoughts before continuing. "I know I've said this before, but I'm not sure I ever really loved Heather. She's a great girl, don't get me wrong. Even when we first met, she liked me. And girls, women, whatever, don't usually notice me, so I, uh, played along I guess. Pretended, which is all I've ever really known how to do. I figured at some point I'd start to feel something for her. But five years passed and nothing changed. It's like no matter what, I always just feel the same. Just cold and distant most of the time. And being with me is ruining any chance she has of finding real happiness." *What do I know about real happiness, anyway?* "I hope that one day she finds someone who loves her. Someone . . . who isn't like me. When it comes down to it, I've always treated her like more of a roommate than anything else."

The fifteenth of June was coming, and the thought of it struck Drew all at once.

"She usually comes with us to see Mom every year. I don't relish the thought of entertaining Logan on my own. He's such a smug, arrogant prick. Thinks he's so much higher and mightier than the rest of us."

Three minutes and fifty-two seconds.

"I'd swear Logan blames Dad for Mom's death." Drew bit his fingernails as he spoke, unaware he was doing it. "Oh, uh, I saw Dad this morning. He's coughing pretty bad. I know his health hasn't been great, but . . . I don't know."

He released a deep breath. Four minutes and eighteen seconds. "Oh, I almost forgot. Neil took home some chick from the bar last night." Drew laughed to himself as he recalled the hazy details. "She comes up to our table, right?" He used his hands to imitate a pair of melons on his chest. "So, basically all Neil does is introduce himself, grab her ass, and off they go. No idea how he does it."

Four minutes and thirty-seven seconds.

"I mean, I dated Ashley for a bit before I met Heather. But I've never really been all that forward with women. There was Julie at senior prom. But, uh, I never really got any practice talking to women as an adult." He looked hard at himself in the video preview. *Probably because I'm goofy looking.* "But I'm okay with being on my own. I mean, I kinda like the idea of being alone. Takes the pressure off."

Even after all these years keeping a diary, Drew often felt as though he was lurking in the shadows, describing his own life from a distance, unsure what was worth noting. Should he share his thoughts and feelings, or just stick to facts? How honest should he be? He wanted to like himself, after all.

Five minutes and two seconds.

"Well, those are my updates. I hope Heather forgives me. I don't . . . I *don't* want her back. I just want her to be okay with us being apart. It's what's best for both of us." *Is it?* "She deserves to be happy." *Don't I?* "And, uh, not that I believe in God or any of that life after death stuff, but I'm not really sure what my next move will be. I—" Drew hesitated. His next thought felt too raw to speak out loud. "I wish Mom could somehow talk to me. To tell me what my life was supposed to be. What I need to do next. Like, my destiny . . . or something like that."

Five minutes and fifty-two seconds.

Drew stopped the recording and watched as his laptop processed the file, encoding it to his hard drive. There it was—a video file named after the date and time. A moment of his life captured, likely never to be heard or seen again. Just soulless fragments of data stored within a conspicuously labeled folder: Special Moments.

He sat back on his chair for an instant, rocking it, enjoying the fortified solitude of his domain. He glanced at his boxes and wondered if he should start unpacking. *I should probably get some furniture first.* He glanced down at the discarded frame beside his chair. He slowly brought it to his face and scrutinized the photo of Heather, examining her features, confirming his emptiness. He undid the four clasps on the back of the frame and gently removed her portrait. Beneath it was an old black and white photo, creased, torn, and yellowed, which captured him blowing out five candles on a magnificent cake—double chocolate, homemade, and shaped like a race car. His mother had her hands outstretched, holding the cake in front of him, beaming him a wide and joyous smile.

Drew closed his eyes and went back in time. Things were simpler. His mother was alive. His father was happy and healthy. And Logan was too young to be condescending. He stood up and grabbed his keys and wallet. He took off in search of his favorite bottled mistress, making sure to lock the door this time.

Chapter 5

Drew awoke Monday morning on his bare mattress to synthetic chimes. He grabbed his phone from beside his head and swiped the noise away. Lesser men might have lingered in bed after what his liver had processed overnight, but he had always been an early riser, no matter how little he slept or how much he drank. He walked from his living room to the bathroom and trimmed his overgrown stubble into something uneven, albeit intentional, before hopping in the shower.

His bedroom was empty aside from the closet, its floor piled high with wrinkled garments. Throughout his years in sales, he had acquired an extensive wardrobe. It wasn't that Drew prided himself on appearance—most of his professional attire was cheap and poorly fitted—but he did pride himself on sealing the deal.

Sales had always felt like a game to Drew. A chance to prove that he wasn't totally inept at conversing with others, even if he didn't enjoy it. It was also a means to quantify his success, as if each sale validated that he wasn't a complete antisocial outcast.

He chose a striped shirt and solid gray slacks. He walked into the kitchen and glanced at the counter—a plate, a knife, a plastic straw cut in half, and a small mountain of white powder. It called to him.

He thought of the day before, setting out to pick up a few essentials for his new home—groceries, soap and toothpaste, toilet paper, and half a gram of cocaine.

"Bro, I'm not your fucking dealer," Neil had said when Drew showed up at his door.

"I know. But you've got some. Hook me up."

He motioned for Drew to keep his voice down. "I stock coke for the ladies. Some of them want a bump before we get busy."

Drew hadn't wanted to beg. "Can you help me out this one time?"

"Fine." Neil vanished into his condo and returned seconds later. "Here you go," he said, placing a small baggie in Drew's hand. "This is good shit, bro. Enjoy."

Drew handed Neil forty dollars.

"You're short."

"I'll get you the rest," he said.

Drew returned to the moment, straw in hand. *Do I wanna get fired from this job, too? Before I'm even hired?* He pushed the desire for a pick-me-up from his head. He grabbed a couple of cereal bars from the cupboard and sprinted out the door.

* * *

Drew pulled into a parking lot in front of a long stone building. It had once been home to a large retailer but had since been bought out and rebranded. Erected across a strip of freshly cut grass were dozens of street-facing signs with neon lettering, announcing, Job Fair Today.

He looked up at a banner stretched above the main entrance indicating that this was now Transtel, A Global Leader In Communications. *More like the only call center outside of India.*

The building was quiet except for murmurs that seeped through a glass pane that overlooked the call center floor.

Workstations were plastered with vibrant motivational gibberish—quotes about teamwork taken out of context from the Dalai Lama, and uplifting phrases starting with each letter of words like attitude, positivity, and happiness. College students, single moms, retirees, and other members of society's most disenfranchised answered calls with insincere enthusiasm. Drew took it all in with cynicism.

A mousy voice arose from over his shoulder. "Are you here to speak with a hiring manager?"

Drew spun around to find a middle-aged redhead, cross-eyed with thick glasses, and one disproportionately large front tooth. "Uh, yes, I am."

"Okay then, sir," Bucktooth said, leading Drew down a wide corridor. "Right this way."

He followed her into a waiting area. Colorful plastic chairs lined the outside of the room, most of which were filled with anxious job seekers waiting to plead their cases. Most of them looked as unhappy to be there as they were unqualified to do much else.

"Have a seat, sir," Bucktooth said.

Drew nodded. "Of course. Thanks." He chose the closest empty chair.

Assigning nicknames to perfect strangers was not only a fun way to pass time, it was also a lot easier for Drew than learning given names. He glanced around the room and caught sight of a mass of skin and bones—a woman no older than Drew. Bones wore a lounge dress and her arms were covered in track marks and tattoos. She brushed a strand of greasy hair from her sour face with a trembling hand.

A few seats to his left sat a young female blowing bubbles in her gum and reading a magazine—something about lip injections. She looked to be barely out of high school. She wore excessive makeup and kicked her feet back and forth, listening to pop anthems through earbuds. *It's gonna be hard for Bubbles to afford cosmetic surgery working here.*

"Daddy—" A shrill whimper pulled Drew's attention to the far end of the room. There sat a young father, desperately working to calm his restless son. The man had a bushy mustache and sported an ugly wool sweater—the type worn as a gag to Christmas parties. His son, a boy no older than eight, wriggled in his seat, pleading for them to go home.

"Daddy needs to speak to someone about a job, Braden."

"But how come it has to be now?"

"Because. Someone is here to speak with me today, and I've got nowhere else to leave you."

"Can't Mommy come get me?"

"No, Braden. We won't be seeing Mommy for a little while."

"But Daddy," he whined. He started bawling and Mustache cupped his hand over the kid's mouth.

Bucktooth returned with a clipboard. "Name?"

"Drew Thomson. That's Thomson without the pea." He stood and extended his hand to shake hers but was interrupted.

"How much longer will it be?" Bubbles asked.

"Not long now, miss."

Drew sat back down. "I'm sorry, I thought this was a job fair of some kind?"

"Oh, sir, it is," Bucktooth replied. "Didn't you grab a brochure on the way in?"

"I can't say I did."

"Well, just ask on your way out—I'll get you one. For now, let's get you in front of a manager. Training starts next week."

The rapid clip-clop of heels shifted their focus to a

THE FIFTEENTH OF JUNE

woman entering the waiting room. She was in her twenties and had vivid green eyes. Her dress contoured to her figure, and her presence commanded attention. Drew couldn't help but stare.

"You here to see a hiring manager?" Bucktooth asked her.

"Yes, ma'am," she said with the kind of energy one might exude after winning the lottery.

"Name?"

"Kara Davenport."

Bucktooth examined Kara from head to toe.

Jesus. Even Bucktooth wants to bone her.

"Have a seat, miss. You'll be called in shortly."

Kara sat next to Drew. She reached into her handbag and pulled out her phone long enough to silence its ringer. She gently placed her bag by her feet and smoothed out her dress with manicured hands before turning to Drew. "Hi," she said.

Why is she talking to me? "Hi," he replied.

"Lots of people here, huh?"

Two young men wearing baggy jeans and matching checkered bandanas entered the reception area. Bucktooth took their names.

"Yeah, almost too many," Drew replied, clearing his throat. "Kara, right?"

She giggled. "Yes, I guess you caught that. What's your name?"

"I'm Drew. Drew Thomson."

"Katrina," Bucktooth called. "Go on in, miss. You're next."

Bubbles scowled and marched over to Bucktooth, who ushered her through a door leading to a small side office. The door shut behind her.

"Kids these days," Drew said with a smirk.

"I know, right?" Kara replied. "What a brat."

Drew inhaled deeply, savoring the allure of Kara's sweet floral-citrus fragrance. As a rule of thumb, he endeavored to keep others at a distance. But Kara intrigued him—and not just because of her good looks. He felt compelled to engage her in conversation despite feeling inadequate and apprehensive. "So, what brings you to Transtel?"

She looked confused. "I need a job."

"You, uh, don't look like someone I would have expected to meet here."

"Oh no?" She raised an eyebrow. "What do I look like?"

"Uh, no, I just meant—"

"Is it because I have all my teeth?"

Drew laughed. "Well, sure, that's part of it."

Kara reached out and straightened Drew's collar. "Are you applying to be the manager or something?"

Her hands lingered around his neck—unexpected and appreciated. Drew felt his groin swell. "Oh, God no, nothing like that." He thought for a moment. "Guess you could say I need a job, too."

"Ever worked at a call center before?"

"Nope."

"You like talking to people all day?"

"No. I hate it, actually." He decided to change the subject. "Any chance you're single?" *Oh, fuck. Way to be tactful.*

Kara suppressed a grin. "Are you always this smooth with women?"

"Yeah, this is as smooth as I get, I'm afraid." Drew forced himself to hold eye contact with her. It felt uncomfortable, but he didn't want his self-doubt to show. "Do interviews make you nervous, too?" He hoped to take the attention off himself.

"A little bit." She hesitated. "Why? Do I look nervous?"

"No. You look great." *Attaboy. Way to dump your girlfriend of five years then find a hotter chick to hit on. Nice moves.* Drew ignored the voice in his head. Apparently everyone had this same little voice, a voice of reason that helped sort right from wrong. But his little voice mostly antagonized him, stressing his insecurities, empowering his anxiety. Yes, he had recently broken up with Heather, but all he was doing was talking to someone—no harm in that, right? At some point he had to move on. This was good practice.

"Was that a compliment?" Kara asked, running her hands through her hair.

"Yeah, uh, I believe it was."

"Thank you, Drew Thomson. You're not so bad yourself."

Drew's cheeks got warm. "Thanks. But seriously, don't be nervous. They're going to hire every person in here."

"How do you know that?"

"Because it's Transtel," he whispered. "They can't hold on to people. Everyone hates it here. Look around—I mean, honestly. What kind of business has a drop-in recruiting day? They're about to interview a guy who could win first place in an ugly sweater contest. Who, by the way, brought his fucking kid to a job interview. They do this same song and dance every month."

Kara looked around the room, her expression shifting between confusion, revulsion, and delight. Drew used reading her reactions as a pretext to examine her body—ears decorated with delicate studs, exposed collarbone, small, perky breasts, a slender waist, and what was most certainly a firm, round backside occupying the seat next to him.

She looked back at Drew. "Welcome to the freak show."

"The interview is just a formality so these guys can tell their clients they screen their staff carefully. But the truth is that they'll take—" Drew thought back to what he had told Neil at The Stone Goblin Friday night, "—anything with tits and a heartbeat."

"That's good to know," Kara said with a smile. "Although I don't have much happening in the tits department. Maybe they'll settle for a fat ass instead."

Drew gulped. "I would." He grew stiff, his erection visible through his slacks. "I mean, not settle. I'd—"

Kara silenced him by placing a finger on his lips. "I think I know what you'd do," she said, glancing down.

Bucktooth welcomed another candidate to the reception area—a man with a limp, a shabby plaid jacket, and stubble too long to be intentional, too short to be stylish. His body odor was severe and unmistakable. Between greeting newcomers, Bucktooth called interviewees to the side office one at a time, the room rapidly turning over its occupants.

Drew strained to think of something clever to say—anything that might charm Kara before his name was called—but came up with nothing.

She spoke first. "So you're telling me that you're applying here because you know you can't fail?"

"Yeah. Something like that."

"Nothing wrong with that, I guess. A job's a job, right? We've all got bills to pay. And it's nice to have a few bucks to go out every now and again. No one wants to sit at home alone—"

"So you are single then."

She gave him a coy smile. "Yes, Drew Thomson. I'm single. You gonna ask me out on a date now?"

Drew shook his head. "No, I need a job first. But," he began, riding a sudden wave of confidence, "if we ever did go out, what would you like to do?"

"Anything you'd like," she replied.

Anything? "Anything?"

"Anything."

He gave his head a shake. "Uh, you like to party?" he asked. Aside from the occasional gathering hosted by Neil, Drew didn't party often—unless getting drunk by himself counted—but he figured Kara was likely an active socialite.

"I like to have fun sometimes. What about yourself?"

Maybe I should tell her how I talk to my webcam on a rocking chair. That'll get her in the mood to party. She'll probably beg me to take her home right this minute. "Yeah, absolutely," he lied.

"Do you smoke?"

"Weed?"

"Yes, weed, Drew Thomson. Do you smoke it?"

Drew glanced to their left and right—no one was listening. "Yeah, I smoke."

"Good. We'll get high sometime."

Bucktooth appeared again. "Drew," she called.

"Knock 'em dead, tiger," Kara said. "Guess I'll see you in training?"

Drew smiled and nodded. He wanted to ask for her number, but wasn't sure how to go about it.

"Drew," Bucktooth called a second time, looking straight through him with her crossed eyes.

Bucktooth closed the door and Drew found himself in the presence of a bald man in his late thirties, who was about seven tons overweight. The buttons on his shirt looked as if they were ready to pop. He extended his hand. "Hi, I'm Paul Yannic."

"Mr. Yannic." Drew shook his hand. "I'm Drew Thomson. Pleased to meet you." He had met hundreds of decision makers over his years in sales—each one easier to manipulate than the last. Fat guys were his favorite. They had so little ability to say no. "You look like a busy man, sir."

"Tell me about it. Going to have to work through my lunch today. And please, call me Paul."

You'll starve by the looks of it. Drew offered a fake smile. "Don't let yourself get too hungry."

Hungry Paul tilted his head to the side, unsure how to take Drew's comment. "Have a seat," he said, waving at the two open chairs in front of his desk. "Did you bring a resume for me?"

Drew opened a suede messenger bag and pulled out two crisp sheets of white paper. He passed them to Hungry Paul.

After taking a moment to review both pages, he looked up at Drew. "This is your resume?"

No, you stupid fucker. I borrowed it from a guy at the soup kitchen like all the rest of the degenerates you talked to today. "Yes, sir. It is."

"Very impressive. How did you enjoy working with The Ascension Group?"

It was lovely. They even let me get high on the job sometimes. "I found my work challenging and rewarding. It meant a great deal to me to exceed my clients' expectations." Drew cherished corporate speak. It was cold, formal, and predictable—second nature, in other words.

"Uh huh. You sold office supplies, right?"

"Yes. The Ascension Group is a distributor for a number of high quality lines of stationery and office supplies. Printers, too. Mostly corporate sales."

Drew could tell that Hungry Paul was many things, but he wasn't completely obtuse. Guys working lucrative corporate sales gigs didn't volunteer to answer phones for minimum wage.

"Why did you leave?"

"If I can be honest, Hung—uh, Paul, I'm ready for a new

challenge."

"You were there three years. You must have been earning—what? Seventy or eighty thousand?"

Yes. "No, not quite that much," Drew said.

"I mean, the job here pays a lot less than that."

"I know. But that's okay. I—" Drew paused. He was prepared to trade financial gain for relative obscurity—a job without stress or consequence. "I have my sights set on management, to be frank. I think I could add a lot of value in a leadership role here. If you'd consider me for management, that is, one day."

Hungry Paul seemed pensive. "Think you could adjust from working outside the office to being confined to a desk all day?"

"Oh, absolutely. If anything, I'd welcome the opportunity to get off my feet for a few hours each day." He hoped to appeal to the limited mobility of his obese interviewer.

"Well, then I'd like to offer you a spot on our team. Training begins next Monday at eight. Welcome aboard."

No other questions? Not even a reference check? You're not even going to tell me what the job is? No wonder this fat fuck can speak to a hundred people a day. "I'm honored, sir. Thank you," Drew said, shaking his hand.

After a short exchange, Drew pardoned himself and returned to the waiting room. He passed Bucktooth then slowed his pace as he approached Kara.

"How'd it go?"

"Perfect. Hopefully I'll see you next Monday."

"I hope so, too."

"Kara," Bucktooth called.

Kara picked up her handbag and made her way to the side office, her scent leaving a trail that Drew committed to memory.

Bucktooth appeared in Drew's field of vision. "Would you still like a brochure, sir?"

"No, thank you. I'll get to know this place soon enough, I'm sure."

Transtel wasn't only a step backward in his career—it was like a colossal backflip off a cliff. No need for a guided tour to see what rock bottom looked like.

But handling irate callers would be easy. Drew knew he'd be able to remain anonymous and intoxicated on the job— and get paid to do both. And if there was any justice in the world, perhaps he would see Kara again, too.

Drew left the building and got into his car. He closed the door and took a moment to appreciate the silence. *This is worth celebrating.* It wasn't only the sense of security in finding a job that Drew intended to celebrate. He had also navigated a successful exchange with an attractive woman.

According to the dashboard, it was just past ten thirty. Drew grabbed a water bottle in his cup holder and brought it to his mouth, swallowing several gulps of vodka. Not his first choice of refreshment, but it had been on sale. And vodka worked as well as any liquor—besides, he'd be home shortly, where there was coke and weed waiting for him.

Chapter 6

Tuesday morning arrived and Drew turned into Hillcrest Cemetery. He took a gulp from his water bottle, carefully navigating his car up a narrow paved path, which wound to the heart of the grounds. He parked behind two familiar vehicles then slowly emerged, carrying a small bouquet of flowers he bought from a nearby gas station.

Expansive rolling hills were decorated with stones of every shape and color—tall pinks, short grays, and variants in between. Some stood upright while others were tilted with age. Faded and forgotten along with grief from decades past. Dark clouds gathered in the distance and there was a light drizzle. The forecast called for a thunderstorm and one was surely brewing.

He climbed a short hill to find Russell and Logan gathered in front of Angela. Both men held umbrellas—a commodity Drew had never thought to acquire for himself. He used his sleeve to wipe water from his brow then approached his mother, laying his bouquet alongside others at her head.

"You're late, Andrew," Logan said.

"Nice to see you, too." Drew stepped under his father's umbrella. "Doesn't look like I missed much."

Russell placed an arm around Drew. "You're here now. S'pose that's all that matters."

"Sorry," Drew said to his father. "Traffic. You know."

Russell nodded. Drew and Logan exchanged hostile glances.

Logan was slightly taller and leaner than Drew, certainly more effeminate. He had a wiry frame, a clean-shaven face, and fair features, like his mother. It was unusually cool for a June day and Logan donned layers of expensive garb, including a double-breasted trench coat and a dainty salmon colored scarf.

"Let's begin," Russell said.

All three men instinctively lowered their heads.

When Angela died, Russell had purchased their plots together—him on the left, her on the right, one companion headstone between them. It was inscribed with both of their names and birthdays, and Angela's date of death, his yet to be added.

"Angie," Russell began, "We're here, my love. All of us."

The Nowaks—Angela's sister and mother—never joined them. The Thomson men had no idea if they were even still alive.

Drew took hold of the umbrella while his father reached inside his jacket, rummaging to locate and open a pack of cigarettes. A dense plume of smoke escaped from Russell's nostrils. He choked for a moment before regaining his composure while Logan glanced at his watch.

"We're all doing well, Angie. Life's treating us good. Your boys are both men now," he said, looking at his sons. "S'pose you'd be proud."

Drew liked the idea of one day being reunited with his mother but often found himself conflicted. His disbelief in an afterlife rendered his father's words meaningless. Then again, Drew used his laptop to converse with an audience of none. He and his father shared that in common—they found solace in talking to themselves rather than others.

"Logan is carving his path in the world, Angie. And Drew," Russell hesitated, taking a drag off his smoke. More coughing. "Well, Drew takes after me."

Logan smirked—as if to silently broadcast his superiority—even though a vote of confidence from Russell was, in all likelihood, worthless to him. The shining example of what no one should ever become.

"Anyway, we all miss you," Russell said. "We know you're still with us and we never stop thinking about you."

"Love you, Mom," Logan added.

After a deliberate moment of silence—interrupted only once by coughing—all three men raised their heads to see who would speak first. Logan volunteered. "You got stuck in traffic, Andrew?"

"That's what I said."

"At eleven in the morning?" Logan asked, as if he were cross-examining an expert witness.

"Yes, Logan." Drew made no attempt to hide his irritation. "It's always congested down by the office. You know that."

"Funny," Logan said, "because I stopped by your office yesterday to meet you for lunch, and it turns out you don't work there anymore."

Drew snorted. "You're a fucking private eye now, too?"

"Drew," Russell interjected, "don't talk like that in front of your mother."

"Thank you, Russell," Logan said. "But before you come down too hard on him, why don't you stomp out that cigarette? It's a bit tasteless to smoke at your wife's grave, isn't it?"

Russell conceded, most likely hoping to placate Logan.

Drew took a long stride and got in Logan's face, their

noses nearly touching. "Back off," he said. "This is a tough day for Dad."

Drew wasn't a fighter—he lacked the physical agility, let alone the drive, but he hoped his tough stance might intimidate his brother. It's not like Logan was built for brawling, either. His diminutive figure put him at a disadvantage.

Logan sniffed. "Is that booze I smell on your breath?"

"So what?"

"It's eleven thirty in the morning. That's what. You show up late to visit mom, couldn't be bothered to shave, you're drunk, and—what? It's no big deal?"

"It's no big deal," Drew repeated.

"It is a huge deal, Andrew. You need help."

The precious few who had ever truly known Drew might have described him as introverted, subdued, or perhaps even quiet. Sure, he had addictions. But none—not even Neil or Heather, who knew him best—would have said Drew was quick to anger. A pacifist under most circumstances, largely the result of a narrow range of emotions, but mostly because he couldn't be bothered. But Logan managed routinely to claw his way under Drew's skin, to get into his head. Drew gritted his teeth and grabbed his brother's scarf, tightening it around his throat. "Let's talk about you instead, huh? How about that? Maybe you're the one who needs help. You show up to see Mom dressed like a fucking faggot. Why? To show her what a little bitch you are?"

Logan wrestled free from Drew, dropping his umbrella in the process. "That's not—"

"Why don't you tell her how you spend your days sticking up for rapists and killers—like the one that got her? I bet she'd be really proud of that."

Russell put his hand on Drew's shoulder. "That's enough."

Drew bucked his father's grip.

Logan raised his hands defensively. "Calm down, Andrew."

"Calm down?" Before Drew could contain himself, he swung his fist. Logan tumbled backward, clutching his nose. "Do you even remember her, or are you too wrapped up in your own life?"

Logan stared up at Drew from the ground, his expression a mixture of pain and contempt, preoccupied more with his ruined attire than the blood dripping from his nose. He scrambled to get back on his feet, but Drew drove his foot into Logan's ribs, causing him to topple. Logan moved again, laboriously, making a second attempt to rise. He lunged at Drew and they both went down.

Russell watched from a distance, his head bowed—as if to silently apologize to Angela—dropping his umbrella and retrieving another cigarette, his thick beard collecting raindrops.

Drew had his brother pinned beneath him, both men covered in mud, raising his fist for another strike. He stared into Logan's face and, for the briefest of moments, saw his mother staring back. Drew lowered his knuckles and got up.

"Jesus Christ, Andrew," Logan said, panting. He stood and looked at Russell for support. "You're not going to say anything?"

"You two are big boys." Russell raised his umbrella back over his head. "Work it out yourselves like real men."

Drew collected his thoughts. "I got fired. That's what happened."

Logan squinted. "Let me guess. You were drunk on the job?"

"High."

"You told me you got laid off," Russell said. He flicked

ash from the end of his smoke with damp hands.

"Laid off. Fired. What's the difference?"

"There's a big difference," Logan said. "Seriously, Andrew. You're out of control. I mean, who acts like this? You need professional help."

Drew took a step toward Logan, causing him to cower. "You'd love one more reason to feel bigger than me, wouldn't you?"

"That's not what I want. What I want is for you to get your life together. Look at you. You lost your job—and not a bad job, I might add. You moved, from what I hear, into a roach infested hellhole around Palmer Heights."

"There's nothing wrong with where I live."

"You dumped Heather—"

"If Heather's so precious to you, have at her. She's all yours."

"That's not what—"

"I'll tell you what, Logan. I'll live my life. And you can go fuck yourself."

Russell pitched his cigarette butt into the damp grass a few feet away. He sighed with an audible rumble and again bowed his eyes to Angela. "I swear it wasn't always this way," he said.

Logan blinked a few times as he processed the scene before him. "I'm glad Mom's dead."

"Excuse me?" Russell replied.

"You heard me, Russell. I'm glad she isn't alive to see this."

Russell wanted to object to Logan's remark but couldn't; he was having another respiratory episode.

"I'm gonna get going," Drew announced. "It's been a blast."

He trotted back downhill to his car, soaked and filthy, but

considered himself the clear victor. His hand throbbed but it was worth it. After closing the car door, Drew swallowed a half dozen mouthfuls of vodka, breathing heavily between each one. He glanced in the rearview mirror, noticing red scratches across his face. *He scratched me? What a pussy.* Drew started the engine just as thunder clapped in the distance, and the drizzle turned into a heavy downpour. He watched Logan scramble to his car. His father descended the hill behind him with pronounced difficultly, using his umbrella as a makeshift walking stick. *I should have held my tongue for Dad's sake.* But Drew knew he regretted nothing. Sure, it was the one day each year his father saw Logan—but that was Logan's choice. Not his. *I should have—*

He pushed the voice of reason from his head and chuckled to himself. "Got that fucker good. Hope I broke his nose."

All three cars exited Hillcrest single file, down the meandering path and back to the open road. The first two vehicles turned toward town, but Drew decided to make a stop before heading home.

Chapter 7

Drew preferred to gamble online. It was faster, there were fewer distractions, and nobody in his personal space. But his credit cards were maxed and the casino handed out free drinks, so it wasn't a bad alternative. It also happened to be a short drive from the cemetery.

He sat at a roulette table in the company of strangers. Lights flashed and bells rang in every direction, announcing big wins and overpriced thrills—a jarring contrast to the muted faces of his fellow players.

The newest croupier at the table—Theodore, according to his badge—started the roulette ball spinning for the thousandth time. "Place your bets," he said.

Drew slid a short stack of chips on the table, betting them on black.

Casino odds came easily to Drew. They made perfect sense even when he was drunk. He knew the house had an edge. In that sense, Heather wasn't wrong about his gambling—over the years, he had come out behind more often than not. But every now and again, he brought home a good haul. And she had never found reason to complain when *that* happened.

The ball bounced to a halt. "Red, five," Theodore said, wiping the table clean of chips.

There were no clocks in the casino and Drew had left his

phone in the car. And unlike his metrosexual brother, Drew's wrist was devoid of a fashionable timepiece.

To his right sat a tall Native American man with long hair. He wore an eye patch and short sleeves that exposed beefy arms and intricate tattoos. "Any idea what, uh . . . what time it is?" Drew asked, hearing himself slur his speech.

Pirate was fixated on some blackjack players a few tables over.

"Uh, excuse me," Drew said, tapping him on the shoulder.

He acknowledged Drew at last. "Asians. Fucking love their casinos, don't they?" Pirate was somehow more inebriated than Drew.

"They do?"

"Yeah," he confirmed. "They all come here together on tour buses. Just look around you."

Drew scanned the vicinity. There were a lot of Asian people. But there were plenty of broke and desperate white folks, too—particularly the fat and old variety—strapped into machines through reward cards. "I thought your people were the big casino buffs."

"No, it's the Asians. I'm telling you. Like that guy," he said, pointing out a middle-aged man playing blackjack. "Gambling powerhouse and, uh, kung fu master probably. That chink is in here every week."

"How do you know that?"

"Because I'm here every week."

The pot just called the kettle . . . chink?

The ball started rolling again. Drew mechanically placed another bet on black.

A haggardly server, the type who had to work hard for tips, brought Drew the beer he had ordered. "Thanks," he said, handing her a dollar bill.

"At the rate you're going, you're gonna put my kids through college," she replied.

"Barber college, maybe." Drew snickered then wondered why he had said it. *That was mean, even for me.*

"Red, thirty," Theodore announced. Drew lost again.

"You been working this table for hours and don't got nothing to show for it," Pirate said. "You must know something I don't."

"Always bet on black," Drew replied.

"But your odds are only fifty-fifty."

"Forty, uh, wait . . . forty-six percent, actually. Yeah."

"So you lose more often than you win," Pirate deduced, flexing his elementary math skills.

"You never lose. It's called Martingale betting. Just double your bet each time red comes up."

Theodore glared at Drew. A betting system wasn't the same thing as cheating, but it was frowned upon regardless.

Pirate squinted, training his eyes on Drew's diminished stack of chips with some effort. "Looks like it's working out just great for you."

Theodore announced the ball was again on the move.

Maybe coming here hadn't been such a great idea. Drew had walked in forever ago with less than two hundred dollars, which was all the cash he had left until payday. Then again, it was so little—what did he have to lose? He had been up on slots, down on blackjack, back up on poker, and then settled into roulette for the remainder of the night.

"Of course," Drew admitted, "I could run out of chips if it hits red a bunch of times in a row."

"And you can only double your bet so many times. You'll hit the table limit sooner or later, and then you're fucked."

Drew hated to admit that Pirate was right. "Fuck it," he said with force, pushing the remainder of his chips on the table. "Been up and down all night. Let's do this."

A second later, Theodore gave a dismissive wave of his hand. "No more bets," he called.

The ball stopped spinning.

"Black, twenty," Theodore announced.

"Holy shit," Drew whispered.

"How'd you know to bet on twenty that time?" Pirate asked.

Because I'm psychic, you fucking moron. "Magic," he replied. "Actually, Mom died twenty years ago today."

Pirate's jaw dropped.

"Well, yesterday now, I guess—I don't know," he admitted. "I'm not even sure what time it is."

"It's about five thirty in the morning, sir," Theodore said, sliding Drew his winnings.

Jesus Christ! "Say that again?"

"Five thirty, sir."

"You don't say." Drew turned to Pirate. "Enjoy your night—uh, morning." He nodded and Pirate returned the gesture.

Drew removed himself from the table and paid a short visit to the cashier's window. He was uneasy on his feet, acutely aware of his own intoxication, but attempting to hide it, as most alcoholics do. In all, he would be leaving the casino with just over fourteen hundred dollars. It was by no means a jackpot but certainly a much needed windfall. Probably more than he'd get on his first check from Transtel.

Drew staggered to the parking lot, disappointed to find his water bottle dry. He sat still for a moment, composing his thoughts, steadying his hands on the wheel. He considered taking a nap before driving home, but decided that beating rush hour traffic sounded much more appealing. With a turn of the key, he was off.

Chapter 8

The sun was rising as Drew pulled in to visitor parking. He entered his building through the back door and proceeded to the lobby.

A man called out to him from further down the grimy hallway. "Mr. Thomson?"

Drew recognized the voice. It was the superintendent, Mr. Patel. He was a gaunt Indian man embellished with suspenders, socks and sandals, and a pair of bifocals secured with a shoestring. His accent was hardly noticeable, but enough to amuse Drew.

"Morning, Mr. Patel," he replied. "You're looking dapper."

"Oh. Thank you, sir." Patel lowered his voice. "I must speak to you about where you park your car."

"What about it?"

"I see you park outside but you have a spot in the underground parking."

"Yeah, well, the clicker doesn't work."

"Ah, okay. I'll get you a new clicker."

"You do that. But right now, I need some sleep." Drew pressed the button to call the elevator.

"There is one other matter, Mr. Thomson. A couple days ago, I was on your floor and I smelled marijuana as I approached your door."

A young man wearing a beanie, mammoth ear spacers, and skater shorts entered the lobby. He watched each floor number light up as the elevator descended but pressed the button five or six more times for good measure.

"Impossible," Drew replied.

Patel bobbled his head. "Oh, but I am one hundred percent sure it was coming from your unit."

"Maybe you should install better doors," he said. "You know, to lock smells in. There's this Paki family on my floor and when they cook, it stinks. Think you could have a word with them for me?"

The elevator door opened. A handful of tenants got off. Drew entered and pressed ten. The young man waiting with Drew entered and pressed nineteen four times.

"This is your only warning, Mr. Thomson. If I catch you with drugs, I'll call the police."

I hope they bring donuts. "Sure thing."

The elevator door closed and it began to move.

"You do drugs?" the young man asked.

"Leave me alone."

"No, for real. I deal a bit on the side."

"The side of what?"

"School."

Drew looked him up and down. "You're in school?"

"College," he replied. "Fine arts."

You've got to be kidding me.

He leapt for Drew's hand, giving it an overeager pump. "Pleased to meet you. I'm Marcus, and I live in this building, too."

"I gathered that."

Marcus leaned in to Drew as if to tell him a secret. "So what do you need?"

"Right now, I need you to get out of my face."

The door opened at the tenth floor. Marcus followed Drew. "Come on, man. I just heard the Indian guy say you like getting baked. You got a connection or what?"

Drew stopped at his apartment door. He had a contact near his old address—now Heather's apartment—but nothing convenient. Neil was his only connection to the heavier stuff, and it seemed he didn't enjoy sharing. "What exactly can you get me?"

"What are you into?"

"Weed, blow, Russian whores—"

"Girls I can't do—"

"I was kidding."

"But anything else, just tell me what you need and I'll bring it to you."

Drew groaned. "Fine. Bring me a half ounce."

"Half an ounce of weed?"

"No, cocaine." Drew paused for effect but Marcus didn't seem to catch on. "What kind of drug dealer are you? Yes, weed. If I could afford half an ounce of coke, I wouldn't live here."

"Right. Half an ounce of weed. Got it."

"But bring it by sometime this afternoon. I need to shut my eyes for a bit." He entered his apartment and locked the door behind him.

Drew grabbed his grinder and some rolling papers off the windowsill. He rolled a small joint from the bud he had left. He was tired but somehow found his mind alive, still exhilarated from his win earlier that morning.

"Mr. Thomson," Drew said out loud, doing his best Indian accent. "You mustn't smoke marijuana. It is disturbing your neighbors." He laughed at his own absurdity, motivated both by fatigue and drunkenness. "Sounds like Marcus is okay with it." He went to spark the joint but paused.

Fucking Patel. Drew took his only two towels from the bathroom and placed one at the base of each doorway, barricading the exits to the hallway and his balcony.

A quick flick of his lighter and—finally—Drew sank into a moment of perfect isolation. He parked himself on his mattress, inhaling deeply, treasuring the sensation, and replaying the past twenty-four hours in his head. Plenty had happened that he would need to record in his video diary, but it would have to wait.

* * *

Forceful rapping reverberated throughout the apartment. The afternoon sun beat down on Drew's face. He awoke slowly and made his way to the door, kicking away the towel, and then leering through the peephole. *Marcus.* He opened the door and greeted his guest with a blank stare.

"Can I come in to complete our transaction?"

"You're, uh, pretty stealthy for a drug dealer."

Marcus walked in and surveyed the empty space. "Did you get robbed or something?"

"I'm a minimalist. You got something for me or not?"

Marcus extended his hand, presenting a baggie.

"What do I owe you?"

"A buck fifty."

"I don't even know if this shit's any good."

"All right, fine. Buck twenty."

"Are you new at this?"

Marcus tittered, oblivious to the insult. "I've actually been doing this for a little while."

"Looks like it." Drew fished his casino winnings from his pocket and counted out payment.

"Right on," Marcus said, placing the bills neatly in his wallet. He retrieved a business card and handed it to Drew.

"What's this?"

"My card."

"You have a card? With your actual phone number on it?"

"Yeah, it says I'm a tutor."

Drew's phone rang. "I gotta get this," he said, motioning for Marcus to take his leave.

"All right, well, just call me if you need anything."

The door shut behind him and Drew grabbed his phone on the third ring. It was his father calling. *From his cell phone?* When Russell left the house—infrequent as that was—he carried a prepaid cell phone with him for emergencies. He rarely turned it on, preferring to use his landline when he got home.

"Dad?"

"Hi, Drew." His father sounded feeble, unclear.

"Is everything okay?"

"Not exactly. I'm at the hospital, Mercy Vale. I've been admitted and—s'pose you could swing by this afternoon?" He muffled the mouthpiece as he hacked in the background.

"Yes, of course." Drew was dumbfounded. "Are you okay? Do you need me to bring you anything?"

"No, just—if you can get ahold of Logan, let him know I'm here. You'll find me on the fifth floor."

"Got it." He darted into the kitchen and sniffed what little coke he had left. He grabbed his keys and flew out the door.

Chapter 9

A wide elevator door opened with a chime, a robotic voice announcing Drew's arrival on the fifth floor of Mercy Vale Hospital. He stepped off and approached a congested nurses' station. A petite woman with matted hair and glossy lips greeted him.

"I'm Drew Thomson," he announced. "I'm here to see my dad."

"Russell Thomson?"

"Yeah, that's right."

"He's anxious to see you," she replied.

"But the sign on the elevator said this is the cancer ward. That can't be right."

"It is."

"There must be some mistake," Drew glanced at the laminated identification pinned to her scrubs, "Holly. Dad is fine. I saw him just yesterday."

"I know this must be difficult." Her empathy seemed rehearsed, indifferent. "But let's go see your dad."

She led Drew through a labyrinth of hallways, moving unexpectedly fast for having such short legs, and he struggled to keep pace with her.

He had always made a point of avoiding hospitals. The last time he had visited one, it had been with Heather two years before. She had broken her ankle on a girls' weekend skiing trip with the Indiscreet Elite. Her anguish was a trivial detail to Drew. He was forced to endure the emergency room followed by the intensive care unit. It felt like he was there for an eternity. Agonizing hours spent alongside suffering babies, crying children, miserable adults, and a whole host of other invalids and incurables. The wretchedness of his surroundings was rooted as much in emotional as physical distress, each patient bubbling with a mixture of pain and grief.

As far as Drew was concerned, hospitals were chambers of desolation cloaked in the suffocating stench of polyvinyl chloride and diluted bleach. They were tombs for the hopeless, asylums for the irredeemable, and homes for the terminal.

"Your father is ill, Mr. Thomson—"

"Call me Drew. He's Mr. Thomson."

"Right. He's asked to speak with you before I say more." Holly stopped all at once, knocking on an opened door to announce their arrival. "Mr. Thomson, your son is here to see you."

Drew entered the room warily. There were two beds, only one of which was occupied. Russell sat upright in the one closest to the door, watching a muted television on the opposite wall. His privacy curtain was pulled back to reveal intravenous lifelines flowing into his body, tubes of oxygen plugged into his nostrils, and a heart rate monitor that beeped callously at his side.

"Drew," Russell said. "Come here, son."

"Press the call button if you need anything, Mr. Thomson," she said.

"I will, but," he coughed, "just call me Russell."

Holly forced a smile. "I'll do that." She left Drew alone with his father.

"Dad, what's wrong?"

Russell launched into a fit of coughing, his belly heaving. "Nothing is wrong, Drew. I'm sick, that's all. And they won't even let me smoke in—"

"You're in the cancer ward, Dad."

Russell lowered his head, evidently numb to the gravity of his present situation. "I've got cancer," he said at last.

"So they're starting you on chemo or radiation or something?"

"No."

"Surgery?"

"No, son. It's too late for that."

"Then what now?"

"We wait," he said, taking Drew by the hand. "The cancer's in my lungs and it's already spread to my stomach and brain."

Drew felt his eyes well up.

"This is my last stop, Drew. It's—it's just a matter of time now."

"How much time?"

"Months, weeks maybe," he hesitated, "or days even. There's really no way of knowing."

Drew thought of his mother. When she died, he had no choice but to come to terms with it. It had happened without warning, without offering his young mind a chance to prepare. But having to accept that his father would soon die, inevitably and inescapably, seemed unfathomable.

"S'pose all they can do now is try to make me comfortable." Another violent cough. "I didn't want to tell you over the phone. I'm sorry you have to see me like this, but—"

"Are you in pain?"

"Tell you the truth, I've been in pain for years. Breathing has always been hard and, well, damn near impossible most days. I just never could be bothered to get it looked at."

"So why now?"

Russell looked toward the window. "Angie called to me at the cemetery, son. I saw her face. She told me it was time to join her."

Drew shifted uncomfortably. He wondered if fantastic delusions were a symptom of cancer, or if it was a simple matter of his father seeing what he wanted to.

"She said you and Logan don't need me no more."

His room looked out on Northwood Park, which was adjoined to the hospital campus by an antiquated wooden bridge. Its picturesque landscape poured through the open blinds, an acrimonious reminder of better days—at least for those patients cognizant enough to appreciate its juxtaposition. Joggers, moms with strollers, and families walking dogs occupied its grounds. Young children played tag, chasing one another around mighty trees, emanating liveliness for all the world to see. But Northwood Park took on a very different meaning for the Thomsons—in its depths is where Angela had met her untimely end so many years before.

Holly resurfaced at the door. "Let's give you a little something for the pain." She approached Russell with a cart full of patches and potions.

Drew looked skeptical. "What are you going to give him?"

"A mild sedative and something to ease his breathing."

"It's okay," Russell said, offering little comfort to his son. He looked strangely at home on medical death row, filled with purpose, peace, and belonging. As though it were where he wanted to be.

Holly worked her methodical magic, likely having cared for oncology patients for years. Many of whom had probably been palliative, resigned to face their undignified demise in a room like this one. She completed her intricate tasks then vacated the room with haste.

Russell winced as the medicine began to course through his veins. He coughed into his pillowcase, projecting a fine mist of blood. Drew handed his father a Kleenex from the bedside table and Russell wiped his mouth.

"Did you manage to reach Logan?"

"I texted him on the way over."

"I've made a lot of mistakes in my life, son."

Hot tears tumbled down Drew's face. "Don't talk like that. You can still fight this." But the words felt forced and clichéd. Russell wasn't the type to come back against the odds, and Drew knew it. His tenacity had perished along with his wife years ago.

"There's nothing left to be done," Russell declared. "I lived my life, and I'm ready to be with your mother again. That's just how it is."

But I'm not ready to be without you. "What am I supposed to do when you're gone?"

Russell took a deep and painful breath. "S'pose this is the part where I give you some words of wisdom, right?"

Drew nodded. Not because he expected to be enlightened, but because he desired to create a moment he could later look back on. Then again, Russell wasn't keen on giving fatherly advice. The few times he had in the past, Drew tuned most of it out. But he felt drawn to his father at that instant, as though a piece of him were lying in the same hospital bed.

"Well, I don't have much to offer." The intravenous elixirs were beginning to take effect—Russell looked drowsy. "The big one, I guess, is don't work too hard. Matter of fact, don't work any harder than you've got to. Someone else will always pick up the slack."

"Uh, okay."

"We all owe one death in this life, son." His eyelids were gaining weight. "There's no need to fear it. It all ends one day, and then we get to rest at last."

"That's your advice?"

"It's what I've got."

"It sounds like you're giving up."

"I gave up a long time ago, if I'm being honest. But it wasn't always this way . . . " Russell faded into peaceful rest, the rhythmic beeping of his heart serving as evidence that his soul remained earthbound, at least for now.

Drew stood still, unsure of whether to remain at his father's bedside or take his leave. Russell was gasping, his chest battling for air. He heard footsteps behind him.

"Andrew," Logan said.

"Look who's late now, asshole. He's already asleep."

"That's okay. A nurse brought me up to speed when I arrived." Logan's voice was somber, and his otherwise pretty face was scraped and bruised from their tussle in the cemetery.

Brought you up to speed? This isn't a deposition. "What kept you?" Drew asked.

"If you must know, I was at an important briefing. I got here as soon as I could." He made eye contact with Drew. "Are you going to hit me and call me a faggot again?"

"No, but I'll tell you this—I wish it were you in that bed instead."

Logan curled his swollen lower lip and nodded, accepting his brother's bitterness with composure. He reached out to their father, brushing back his mop of straggly white hair.

Chapter 10

"I don't think I'll ever understand why Logan and I are so different. We grew up in the same house with the same parents—well, the same dad at least. Even went to the same high school for a while and, somehow, that fuck—I don't know."

The words usually came to Drew in a natural flow. Even at times when he felt compelled to omit his truest thoughts, his darkest inclinations. He had pulled his beaten up rocking chair out on the balcony and rested his laptop on his legs, the clear moonlight enveloping his face. It created a dissonant effect on the screen—as though his face were that of a pale apparition shrouded in darkness.

"And now, what? Logan shows up and pretends he gives a shit about Dad when he was never there." A gulp of beer. "Took off at sixteen like he was fleeing a warzone or something."

Recording an entry in his video diary while drunk wasn't a challenge. Years of dedication and practice had strengthened his tolerance, and keeping his intoxication undetected while functioning at a high level was his specialty. But tonight was different. Drew teetered on the brink of confronting his fears and insecurities, or simply drinking to escape them all. To go on a bender of unforeseeable magnitude, pushing the line between inebriated and comatose. His best failsafe was to avoid liquor in favor of beer. Try as he might, no amount of ale could incapacitate him.

He crushed his empty can, tossing it to the balcony floor, on top of eight or nine others. He grabbed another from a six-pack near his feet, popped it open and chugged half the can.

Drew recalled his younger years. In a world where appearances counted, he had been portly and lacking in style, his hair seldom cut or washed, his clothing secondhand and tattered. He had never been popular in a desirable sense. His peers knew who he was and some even found his cheerless nature comical, but for the most part, he was labeled a relative nobody. An acquaintance of total insignificance. A disheveled and pimply nonentity without a cause. In time, Drew came to accept these traits as core elements of his identity, damning as they were.

His first kiss happened at age sixteen and by total accident. At his first high school party where alcohol was involved, his peers played a game they had devised that involved lining up the boys on one side of the room, the girls on the other. The lights were turned out, and without saying a word, they had seven seconds to choose a partner from the opposite side of the room. The lights remained off for a full minute after, allowing each newly formed couple a private moment together.

It was on the third round that Drew received some uncoordinated tongue action from a cute girl in his grade. When the lights came back on, she was horrified—a case of mistaken identity. Drew felt oddly gratified and embarrassed all at once. In darkness, he wasn't so different from everyone else.

Internet porn aside, he didn't see—let alone touch—a real set of boobs until the following year. Olivia Woods, well known at school for her developed chest, had been an obvious choice to invite to his seventeenth birthday party. He had never actually talked to her, but he had fantasized about her more than once.

For some reason, she had showed up. Toward the end of the night, she followed Drew into the kitchen on a dare, a small group of her teenage girlfriends peering around the corner and giggling. She surprised Drew with a flash of her bare breasts. She eventually agreed to let Drew cop a feel, then—after some coaxing—they relocated to his bedroom and she went down on him. Drew was certain they had an audience outside his door. When he came, Olivia had gagged, spitting his ejaculate all over her lap. She was, after all, just as inexperienced as he was.

Then he remembered prom. Although Drew had no official date, it was an unspoken rule that all high school seniors—who had not done so already—had to lose their virginity that night. The pressure to convince a young lady to drop her panties was almost overwhelming. Drew considered staying home, but decided to go at the last minute. He outfitted himself in a checkered suit jacket borrowed from his father's closet. It looked like something a clown might have worn.

In the wild, animals were known to target weak and sick prey, bettering their odds of a kill. Drew followed their lead, stalking Julie Blair for the night—an above average student with below average looks and nonexistent self-esteem. He brought her punch which, unfortunately, no one had spiked. They danced for an hour or two with all the coordination of an epileptic seizure. They had nothing in common to talk about. Drew was running out of time and too intimidated to make the first move. At the end of the night, Julie cornered him. "We can have sex if you want to," she said with a sheepish grin. "Just don't tell anyone."

They made their way to Drew's car at the edge of the parking lot—also borrowed from Russell—climbed in the backseat, and undressed in deafening silence. He fumbled to open the condom wrapper and get it on, and because he was confused and under pressure to perform, he used the darkness as cover to slide in without it.

Seconds later after only a few clumsy thrusts, the ordeal was over. Julie, who looked too relieved to express her discomfort, got dressed with haste and left. Drew sat naked in the backseat for an hour, wondering what all the fuss had been about.

In his early twenties, prior to working with The Ascension Group, Drew had started down the slippery slope to alcoholism. One night, when he was at a bar by himself, a tipsy and ordinary college girl bumped into him, spilling his drink all over his shirt. She offered to have it dry cleaned for him.

A few days later, she arrived at Drew's door to drop the shirt off as promised. Just as she was about to leave, she asked, "Are you free this Friday by chance?"

"Uh, I think so," Drew had replied.

"Would you let me buy you a drink? I owe you after spilling yours."

"Sure."

"Great. And, well, this is embarrassing," she had said. "I got your phone number and address the other night, but I didn't grab your name."

"Drew."

"Heather."

They shook hands awkwardly and she left.

I wonder if Heather remembers that she once encouraged me to drink.

Despite occasional social achievements—typically the result of dumb luck—Drew had spent most of his teenage and young adult years in the background, floating freely between social settings—unseen, unknown, unavailable. And most importantly, easily forgettable.

By comparison, Logan was widely regarded throughout his high school years as a pretentious nerd. He worked tirelessly at first to fit in. He settled in any socially disenfranchised clique that would have him—the chess team, the book club, the debate team. Logan lived in denial that he was ostracized from ordinary teens. He preferred to think of it as though he were choosing to exclude others from his more noteworthy endeavors—an approach that made him seem cold and snobbish. Girls thought of him as an egotistical loser even back then.

Drew crushed another empty beer can and tossed it aside. He reached down for a new one. Eleven minutes and forty-four seconds had elapsed since he started recording, although most of that footage was his phantom digital face staring into the night sky.

"Thing is, my brother doesn't have to be a two-dimensional cutout. He could be successful in his career and still be a real person, too. You know, like a normal fucking guy." He knocked back a mouthful of beer. "I mean, it's like he picked up one day and just said, 'Fuck it. Fuck all you guys. I'm out.' Then he hit the road and forgot all about Dad, until he got cancer anyway. Just like the rest of the world, I guess—deaf to the good news, all ears for the bad. Soaking up tragedy like a sponge.

"I mean, fuck, the least the guy could do is show up and say, 'Hey Dad. I'm so sorry I was too busy to call for the last ten years. But I'm here now and I'd like to make it up you.' No. Instead, instead that cocksucker strolls in the hospital room like he's doing Dad some kind of favor."

Drew wasn't especially good at being angry. He was far too dismissive of his own feelings to let rage take control. But whenever an exception was made, Logan was surely the cause of it.

He rose swiftly, surprising even himself, his laptop falling to the concrete balcony floor. "That goddamn mother-fucker!" Drew bellowed, tossing his can of beer from the balcony. He heard it thump ten stories below. He dropped his shoulders and let a deep breath out. "I—I needed that."

He picked up his laptop, examining it, discovering it had survived his outburst without incident. *Maybe there is a God.*

Thirteen minutes and twenty-two seconds elapsed. He felt ready to speak again.

"You know what? Fuck him." Drew grabbed another beer and popped the tab. "To be honest, I'm scared. I don't know what I'll do without Dad. He's—he's always been the one consistent thing in my life. Even when I was a teenager and I didn't fit in. He'd tell me, 'Son, if they don't like you, tell them to kiss your ass.' " Drew chuckled. "I'm not sure what I should do—I've got this new job to start at Transtel. But I feel like I should be with Dad. He might need me."

Drew knew that wasn't true. If anything, he needed his father, not the other way around. Russell was mostly taci-turn, unless it came to Angela, and Drew rationalized his own introversion by looking to his father for guidance. Then again, he had to work—professional gambling wasn't a per-manent career choice. Surely his father understood that.

Fourteen minutes and one second.

"So, I'll just go visit Dad when I can," he continued. "And we'll talk on the phone, I'm sure. Maybe, if I'm lucky, he'll stick around for a while." *If I'm lucky? He's suffering. I should be hoping for a swift and painless death.* "I guess right now, I should probably just focus on supporting myself." *Who am*

I trying to convince? "They say a boy doesn't become a man until he loses his father. I guess I'm about to find out if that's true." Drew stopped talking long enough to finish his beer. "Maybe it's time I start thinking about doing something more with my life . . . something more than Dad even thought possible for me."

In truth, Russell had never uttered a discouraging word to Drew. Not that he rooted for his son to change the world. But his father had remained relatively hands off as a parent, allowing Drew to blunder through the blackness on whatever course he chose for himself.

"Who knows? Maybe I'll be just like Logan one day, drowning in my own indignant brand of self-righteous bullshit. But in the meantime, I'm content to live in the moment, day by day. I'm gonna answer phones with the rest of the working poor. And if a caller needs something complicated, I'll just hang up."

Drew recalled his introduction to Kara at the interview. He felt blood rush to his groin at the thought of her.

"I met this chick at the interview named Kara. She's, I don't know—a couple years younger than me, maybe? And she, uh, talked to me. Like actually seemed to not mind me. I mean, she wasn't just fun to talk to. She's stacked. Although I doubt much of anything will happen between us. I mean, she could get her hands on anyone, really." *I found out Dad has cancer and here I am with a raging boner. I'm a special kind of fucked up.*

Fifteen minutes and twenty-four seconds.

"All right, well, that about sums it up. Dad's dying, and I can't do a damn thing about it. Mom's been dead for twenty years now, and I can't change that. Logan's still an asshole, doubt he'll change much. And, uh, I met Kara . . . whose ass I'd like to pound if I ever got the chance." Drew was impressed for a moment with his own vulgar belligerence. His crass remark reminded him of Neil. *Neil . . . now there's a guy Kara would probably fuck.*

"So basically what I'm saying is that life is what it is, and there's nothing I can do to change it. All we get is the present, this one spot in time, and it feels like I'm stuck here."

Fifteen minutes and fifty-nine seconds.

Drew stopped recording, giving his laptop a chance to process his ramblings. He opened Facebook, doing a quick search for the name Kara Davenport. After sifting through the results for a minute, he located her public profile.

Kara Davenport, single, female, twenty-five, over seven hundred friends. Spent the last four years working as an administrative assistant. No education listed. Recent timeline posts include memes about social justice and other do-gooder advocacy bullshit.

Drew clicked over to her photos and scanned through her albums. She looked fashionable and put together in every shot—a full face of makeup, hair done, always in a different outfit. Then he spotted an album of hers labeled: Jamaica.

He clicked through, flipping from one photo to the next. The obligatory airplane selfie. The luggage carousel at the airport. The resort lobby. Photos of the pool filled with random strangers. Kara getting a drink from the lobby bar. Kara hugging a friend. And then—*jackpot!*—Kara at the beach.

In the first photo, she was face down, sunbathing on a chair. The beach was crowded with vacationers, but her flawless legs were the focal point, absorbing rays of golden sun. Her scant bikini was untied across her back and her face was turned toward the camera but covered with a sun hat. The edge of her mouth was visible, her lip curled, as if to give the photographer a shy smile. Somewhere behind her was a local man selling sunglasses on the beach.

In the next photo, she was edging her way into the sea. She posed for the camera, imitating a model with her arms behind her head, her lips puckered, her eyes shielded with what looked like newly acquired sunglasses. Drew's eyes zoomed in on her bikini top, now tied in place, enclosing small and sprightly breasts—delicate, pert, and alluring. She stood with her weight shifted to one side, her backside protruding for examination.

Drew unzipped his pants, taking his erection in hand, balancing the laptop on his knees. He pumped furiously, skipping to the next photo. Kara was on her knees facing the sea, bent over the sand and writing with her finger, her friend from the earlier photo watching her work. The first few letters of Jamaica was all she had managed. Her damp bikini bottoms clung to her hips, tracing silky crevices.

Drew set his laptop on the balcony floor, carefully this time, holding in his mind the image of Kara playing in the sand. He shut his eyes and imagined himself there. Kara slowly slid down her bikini bottoms for him . . .

Just as he was approaching orgasm, he heard a balcony door open below him, footsteps, and several adult voices speaking almost in a whisper.

Fuck, oh no. He couldn't stop. He ejaculated at once, shooting semen to the edge of the balcony. He tilted his head back, hoping to muffle the sounds of his own ragged breathing.

Several moments passed before Drew gathered his remaining two beers and carried his laptop indoors, setting the beers next to his mattress and his laptop on a closed box. He thought of his father for an instant, before turning off the kitchen light and curling in the fetal position on his mattress. Sleep wouldn't come for several hours.

Chapter 11

Transtel was exactly as Drew had left it—dismal and archaic, a gargantuan monument to the broken dreams of the retailer who had previously occupied it. The job fair signs with neon lettering were gone, but they would almost certainly be back one day soon.

He entered the building and peered through the glass pane onto the call center floor. Shift workers rotated positions—some anchoring themselves to workstations to begin their sentences, others collecting their meager belongings, anxious for the arrival of eight o'clock.

In the lobby, an easel stood upright with a message scrawled in permanent marker, instructing all new hires to proceed to the training room. At the bottom was an illustrated arrow, directing Drew down the same corridor Bucktooth had led him for his interview the week before.

The door to the training room was ajar and Hungry Paul greeted him with forced enthusiasm. "Drew, welcome. Please sign in. Grab a name tag and take a seat anywhere you'd like. We'll get started soon."

"Sure thing, Paul. You're doing our training, too?"

"Yeah. I'll be your trainer and your supervisor."

"Wow. Judge, jury, and executioner, huh?"

"What was that?"

"Nothing."

Drew looked around. He was one of the first trainees on scene despite it being ten minutes to the hour. The perimeter of the room was lined with tattered office chairs and computers from the Stone Age. Each chair was turned to face an overhead projector screen at the front of the room. Drew had hoped he might locate Kara and snag a seat beside her, but she was absent.

He grabbed a blank name tag and wandered to the back of the room, taking residence in one of many available spots. Sitting at the back allowed him to blend in while maintaining a clear vantage point over the room. And that meant he could entertain himself for hours with internal dialogue, making inane observations on his fellow misfits.

The training room began to fill with forlorn faces—some crowding in one at a time, others in pairs. Each trainee signed in, adhered a generic name tag to his or her torso, then selected a seat to call home for the day.

Fifteen minutes passed and Drew recognized some familiar characters, although he made no effort to learn their real names. He saw the two guys who had worn matching bandanas to the interview—who Drew decided, for the sake of simplicity, needed nicknames. The first man in a bandana was tall, greasy, and had a thick Italian accent. He was about forty years old. In any other setting, Drew would have assumed he was an automotive mechanic. *Grease Monkey it is.* The other man was short and plump compared to his friend, but about the same age. He had a shrill, sissy voice. No detectable accent but he looked Italian, as well. *Looks just like Super Mario, actually.*

Mustache was noticeably absent. Perhaps he had difficulty finding a caregiver willing to endure alone time with Braden. Kara was still missing, too. Drew was disappointed, though he had no official reason to be.

"It's a few minutes past eight, according to my watch," Hungry Paul said. "So let's go ahead and get started. Welcome, everybody. I'm Paul Yannic—and I believe I met all of you during the interview process." He dimmed the lights, fired up a PowerPoint presentation overhead, and stood round and fat at the front and center of the room.

Like a fucking hot air balloon without the basket.

He began by promising the group that he would cover the job itself, but wanted to begin their first day by reviewing policy. He then droned on for forty-five minutes, articulating everything from what to do in the event of a fire alarm to when it was acceptable to take a bathroom break.

The training room was unpleasantly warm and clogged with the stale musk of human bodies. Drew did his best to sit upright and remain attentive. But between the mugginess, the dimness, the dreary dynamic, and the monotony of Hungry Paul's voice, he found himself fading fast.

The backs of Drew's eyelids featured imagery of a homeless man who had begged him for change that morning. His cardboard sign had read God Bless in large, crisp, black lettering. *Why do bums always have such pristine handwriting? It always looks so fresh and dark, like it was written just hours before with with a brand new Sharpie . . .*

Bubbles made a loud and sudden popping noise with her chewing gum, which startled Drew back to earth but failed to slow down Hungry Paul, who still prattled on.

" . . . just be sure to lock your car doors before you come inside, because Transtel management won't be responsible for . . . "

The training room door swung open and the fluorescent lights in the hallway created an aura that hugged the edges of Kara's frame. She bowed her head toward Hungry Paul in emblematic apology. "I'm so sorry, Paul. I got here as fast as

I could."

"Come on in, Kara—you told me you'd be late. I didn't forget. Go ahead and grab a seat."

She stirred up a commotion, bumping into more than one chair in the dark before settling in next to Drew—one of the few spots still remaining—with a pen and notebook in hand.

Drew couldn't hide his excitement. "You made it," he said softly.

"Good morning, Drew Thomson." She flashed him a demure smile.

He studied her from the corner of his eye. Messy bun, chic blazer, skintight leather pants, and stilettos. She was striking, albeit overdressed for the occasion. But he was seeing Kara in a different outfit, and that meant new material for his spank bank.

" . . . absences not reported to the sick line at least an hour before your scheduled start will be treated as a no-call, no-show, and that means . . . "

Kara leaned toward Drew, secreting the same floral-citrus scent she had worn to the job fair. "Did I miss much?"

"No, not really." He inhaled her with subtlety. "Found out we can only drop out of queue to use the bathroom twice a day outside of regular break times."

"Only twice? What if I've got to pee?"

" . . . all incidents of theft will be grounds for immediate dismissal, and could result in prosecution under . . . "

"You have to hold it until break time, I guess."

"Should we protest?" Kara raised an eyebrow.

"Definitely."

She smirked.

" . . . such incidents will be documented and taken into consideration when completing semiannual performance reviews, so . . . "

"Where were you?" Drew asked. It wasn't like him to follow up, but surely Kara had been somewhere magical and forbidden.

"It's a secret."

" . . . other instances of unacceptable conduct, such as sexual harassment or coming to work under the influence of . . ."

I'm surprised his ankles haven't given out yet.

"All right," Hungry Paul announced at last. "Enough of the boring textbook stuff, right?" Trainees offered up a polite and disingenuous laugh. "You'll each get an employee handbook to review. But for the time being, we're going to do a little icebreaker so we can get to know each other a bit better."

Fuck me.

"This one's called Two Truths and a Lie," Hungry Paul explained. "Have any of you done this one before?" Half the room raised their hands, but he ignored them. "How it works is you'll each take turns telling the rest of the group three things about yourself. Two of them will be true, and the third will be a lie. It's up to the rest of us to guess which one is the lie."

A dark-skinned man with a permanent grin glued to his face—he hadn't stop smiling since training began—tapped his foot and wrung his hands with nervous energy. He cranked his head to the side and discharged a series of rapid-fire tongue clicks.

Press one for English, two for Spanish, or three for Tourette syndrome . . .

The thought of speaking in front of a large group, two dozen or more trainees, seemed to terrify Permagrin, but Hungry Paul didn't notice. He peeped at his watch and said, "I'll give you two minutes to jot down what you're going to say, and then we'll get started." He turned on the lights.

"It's kinda like being back in kindergarten," Drew muttered.

"Oh, come on," Kara teased. "It'll be fun." She tore a sheet of paper from her notepad and ripped it into two pieces, handing one to Drew. "Bet I can guess when you're lying, Drew Thomson."

Why is this chick so fucking sexy? "What are you going to lie about?" he asked.

"You'll have to guess."

"Time's up!" Hungry Paul hollered. "Who'd like to go first?"

A young female trainee raised her hand. Bubbles, as Drew remembered her.

"All right, Katrina. Come on up. Introduce yourself to the room before you start."

Bubbles took the stage with the angst of an adolescent orphan. True to form, she was dressed like an underage prostitute and chomping on a wad of gum.

"Hi, I'm Katrina," she said, waving to the room. "But you probably all knew that."

She's awfully confident. Like a modern day Veruca Salt visiting the Transtel Chocolate Factory.

"Here's what I wrote down," she said. "I used to work part-time as a Disney princess, my favorite Kardashian is Kim, and both my nipples are pierced."

Drew and Kara exchanged glances, confirming they had both heard the same thing.

"Um," Hungry Paul mumbled, "who—who wants to guess the lie?"

Grease Monkey raised his hand first.

"Chris, go ahead. What's your guess?"

"I'll bet you've only got one of those nipples pierced." He

said, licking his lips.

The crudeness of his response wasn't lost on the rest of the room, but Super Mario fist bumped his friend regardless. They both laughed.

Bubbles covered her mouth, her attempt at bashfulness unconvincing. "Nope. They're both pierced," she replied with pride.

Kara raised her hand.

"Kara," Hungry Paul prompted.

"I'm guessing it's the Kardashian thing."

"You got me," Katrina replied with a giggle. "Khloe is actually my favorite."

Kara leaned in to Drew. "Totally not what I meant."

"You're up, Kara," Hungry Paul said.

"The person who guesses correctly goes up next," Hungry Paul said. "But, um, let's try to keep this game appropriate for a professional environment, okay?"

Kara sauntered to the front of the room and Drew followed the hypnotic motion of her leather pants. She offered the room a genuine smile. "Hi everyone, I'm Kara—nice to meet you all."

I think she actually likes meeting new people. Oh well. No one is perfect.

Kara glanced at the note she had scribbled for herself. "Okay, so here are my three things. I took a trip to Jamaica last year, I was a secretary before I started working here, and I was late today because I was at the dentist."

Drew's hand shot up with such exuberance that trainees seated near him took notice.

"Drew, go ahead," Hungry Paul said.

"You weren't at the dentist. That one's the lie."

"You're right," Kara replied, surprised.

She's going to wonder why I was so certain about that.

84

"You're next, Drew," Hungry Paul said.

Kara passed Drew as she returned to her seat, casting an inquisitive glance in his direction.

"Ahem." Drew cleared his throat. "Uh, okay. So, these all happened last week. First I got in a fistfight with my brother at a cemetery, and I won. Then I, uh, won fourteen hundred dollars at the casino that night. And then my dad died of cancer just a few days later."

A distinct gasp arose as trainees traded muddled glances. Even Hungry Paul seemed unsure how to react.

It was unlike Drew to draw attention to himself, but—at that moment—he couldn't be bothered to humor Hungry Paul and his senseless icebreaker.

Grease Monkey leaned back in his chair. "That's easy. The first one. You've never been in a fight in your life."

Super Mario emitted a sharp laugh—more of a shriek—both men oblivious to the uneasiness around them.

"Nope," Drew replied. "And if you think I'm a pussy, you should see my brother."

Hungry Paul grimaced. "Language, Mr. Thomson. Keep it clean." He looked around the room. "Anyone else want to guess?"

Kara raised her hand.

"Sorry, Kara. You already went," Hungry Paul said. "Someone else has to guess now."

A disheveled woman a few feet from Drew raised a gaunt arm. Bones, he had nicknamed her at the interview. "Your daddy ain't dead. If he was, you woulda taken the day off."

Drew nodded. "That's right. He's still alive for now."

Hungry Paul gave Drew a concerned look. "But he does have cancer?"

"Yeah, that part's true. Got it in his lungs. But he's still above ground for now, so that's good." He returned to his seat.

Hungry Paul gave his head a shake. "Um, okay. Well, we're learning lots about each other today, aren't we? Paula, why don't you go next?"

Bones rattled to the front of the room, a tremor evident in her every step.

Drew felt two burning emeralds on the side of his face. He turned his head to find Kara fixated on him, as though she were fascinated by his complexities and imperfections alike.

* * *

At noon they broke for lunch and Drew followed Kara to the cafeteria.

"So your dad has cancer," she said.

"He does."

"That sucks."

"It happens."

"Is it serious?"

"He'll be dead soon."

"Doesn't that bother you?"

"Only on the inside."

Drew wished he hadn't left his water bottle at home. He had assumed his first day of training would require full use of his faculties. But had he known how informal it would be, he would have poured vodka all over his Cheerios that morning.

They entered the cafeteria. A handful of employees trick-led through a sparse line, filling their trays with soggy green beans, tepid French fries, and something that resembled dog food.

I wonder if Hungry Paul spends his whole paycheck in here.

"I lost someone close to me once," Kara said.

"Yeah?"

She pursed her lips. "Taught me to live in the moment. Life is short, you know?"

"I guess. Then again, it's the longest thing we'll ever do."

"Never thought of it that way."

Several vending machines lined the far wall. "I'll be right back," Drew said. He returned with a fistful of candy bars and handed one to Kara. She was seated at one of several long, industrial tables—built like colossal picnic benches— with black coffee in a Styrofoam cup and a buttered bagel. Drew parked himself across from her.

"So," she began, "how did you know I wasn't at the dentist this morning?"

"Because your teeth were already white."

She furrowed her brow. "Seriously?"

He sighed. "You want the real truth?"

"Of course." She sipped her coffee.

"I might have, uh, gone looking for you on Facebook."

Kara fought back a laugh, puckering her lips, straining to prevent an expulsion of hot coffee. She wiped her mouth, transferring nude lipstick to the napkin. "That's too funny."

"Why's that?"

"Because you actually told me the truth."

"I'm a horrible liar."

Kara examined his expression and gave him a knowing smile. "Bet you jacked it, too." She bit into her bagel.

Drew's cheeks got warm. "Did not."

"I told you I'd be able to guess if you were lying, Drew Thomson."

"Fine, maybe I did. Jack it, I mean."

She laughed again, and then made a jerking motion with her hand. "I saw your—" Kara gestured at his crotch through the table, "—bulge at the job fair. You seemed a bit happy to meet me."

"Does that creep you out?"

"God, no. Not at all. I grew up with brothers, a whole house full of boys. It takes more than an erection to scare me off."

"Truth is, I find you exceptionally attractive and I was, uh, hoping to learn more about you."

"That's sweet," she said. "But seriously, you don't have to go undercover. Anything you want to know, just ask." She took another sip of coffee, locking her eyes on his. "What else do you want to know?" Before he could answer, she spoke again. "You're going to ask me where I was this morning, aren't you?"

"Yeah."

"The curiosity is eating you alive, isn't it?"

"It is. Tell me."

Her face turned cold as stone. She placed her hand on Drew's, her palm radiating heat from the coffee cup. "I was getting an abortion."

Drew was speechless. He reserved judgment on that sort of thing. What a woman did with her body was her own business. But it seemed a brazen thing to say, perhaps as outlandish as sharing his father's prognosis that morning.

Kara rolled her eyes with playful indignation. "I'm kidding, Drew Thomson."

"Oh. I mean, it sounded believable. For all I know, you could have been getting your womb vacuumed."

"My womb vacuumed? Jesus. You have a way with words, don't you?"

Drew nodded, as if to accept the compliment.

"You wanna know where I really was?"

"I do."

"I drove my grandma to the cardiologist for a checkup." She patted his hand again. "She's ninety-one and didn't want to reschedule." Kara gave him a second to process what she had just said. "Where did you think I was?"

"No idea." *Good point. What did I expect her to say?*

"My turn," she said. "Which photo did you use to rub one out?"

"Didn't realize we were taking turns at this."

"We don't have to. But I thought you wanted to get to know me better. It'll be more fun if we take turns."

Drew hesitated. "It was the one on the beach."

"The one where I'm bent over, writing in the sand?"

"That's the one."

She grinned. "I should have guessed. Your turn. Shoot."

His mind darted to the indecent—*Does she swallow? What's her favorite position?*—but he'd already confessed to masturbating to her online photos. Something tamer might demonstrate that his interest wasn't purely physical. *She's waiting. Ask her something.* Drew opened a candy bar and finished it in two bites. "Uh, do you want to go smoke some weed?"

She thought for a moment. "Yeah, I do."

In the absence of alcohol, smoking with Kara would be perfect. "I always keep a joint in my glove box. Let's go burn it," Drew said, opening another candy bar.

Kara rocked her head back and forth, deliberating, strands of black hair shimmering in the light. "On second thought, not today. I don't want to end up launching into a giggle fit in training this afternoon. But we'll get high at lunch one day soon. I promise."

"Fair enough—I'd like that. Your turn."

"Wanna go make out instead?"

"Excuse me?"

"Let's go for a walk and find some place private," she said, grinning.

"Like right now?"

"Yeah, like right now."

"You bet. Let's go."

Kara looked like she was about to burst. "I'm joking, Drew Thomson." She held his eye contact. "For now, at least. I just wanted to know what your answer would be."

"I think you already knew what my answer would be."

"I'm sorry. But to be fair, you told me you masturbated while stalking me on Facebook. I'm allowed to have a little fun with you, aren't I?"

He nodded in agreement.

"I like how real you are, Drew Thomson. It's rare and I find it refreshing."

"I try." He thought for a moment. "Will you be honest with me, too?"

"Absolutely. Besides, it's your turn."

"Are you, uh, actually interested in me? Like even a little?"

"I—" Kara looked down and away, as if to dilute her reaction. "I don't deny it. You're good at making me laugh, and that helps." She got up and moved to Drew's side of the table, straddling the spot next to him, a leg splayed on either side of the cafeteria bench. She leaned in—her hands on his thigh—and pressed her lips to his ear. "You want to know something else about me?"

"Sure," he whispered.

"I'm not wearing underwear."

"Wait. Why did you tell me that? Not that I'm complaining." *Hanging around this chick means having never-ending wood.*

Kara grinned and stood up, giving her response consideration. She eventually shrugged. "If you're gonna jerk off again tonight, you might as well have something better to work with than a Facebook photo."

Chapter 12

Russell stirred in his hospital bed.

Drew leaned in, touching his father's arm. "Dad, it's Drew."

"Ah—" Russell moaned in discomfort. "What time is it?"

"Almost six," Drew replied. "I just got off work, my second day."

"How was it?" Russell held his eyes shut but rolled his head toward Drew's voice.

"It was just another boring day of training. Easy stuff."

"That's good. Easy is good . . . "

Drew made a point to visit or call his father daily. He sometimes phoned twice—once at lunch and again in the evening. Logan was predictably absent every time he checked in.

More often than not, Drew arrived to find his father fast asleep. When he called, it almost always went straight to voicemail. Only twice had Drew arrived to find him conscious. Not that he minded—his father was in pain and the main thing was to dispel his agony.

"How are they treating you?"

"Good," Russell replied, his speech a labored grunt. "I feel fine."

The bed at the far end of the room was now occupied by a feeble old man. His privacy curtain was wrapped around him, but he and Drew had exchanged pleasantries the day before. Patrick was his name, if Drew recalled correctly. Patrick was a late stage colon cancer patient. Had his affliction been caught earlier, something might have been done. But aged as he now was, his fate was sealed, much like Russell's—too far gone to successfully recover.

Drew stood at his father's bedside, irresolute on what to say next. He had faded back into restless slumber, his pillowcase stained with a fresh mixture of saliva and blood. The heart rate monitor made its usual racket, an insulting reminder of each absconding moment.

He touched his father's arm again. "Dad."

No response.

"Is that you, Drew?" The voice came from the far bed.

"Yeah, it's me."

"Come over here and say hello."

Drew approached, swiping away the barrier. "Patrick, right?"

The frail man nodded. "That's right, Patrick." Patrick glanced toward Russell. "Your dad and me, we spend most our days out cold. The dope they give us is something else," he chuckled.

I should introduce you to a guy named Marcus… "I was hoping I might keep Dad awake a little longer today and, uh, spend a bit more time with him."

Patrick nodded. "You're a good son. Your father's proud of you."

"He said that?"

"Well—" His eyes shifted, "—not in so many words. But I can tell."

"I, uh, can't shake the feeling that I need something from Dad today. You know, before I lose him. Figured if I could keep him up for a few minutes, I might be able to figure out what that thing is."

"That's natural. Felt that—" Patrick yawned. "Felt that same way when my daddy passed."

Patrick faded back to sleep and Drew returned to his father's side. *Guess you're finally moving on.* "I hope you can hear me," he said. "It feels like I'm stuck in one spot. It's been this way for a long time. I know you understand, but now you're moving on without me. And I—I'm not ready to be alone."

Beep. Beep. Beep . . .

Drew felt like a deer in headlights. He could see the end coming, but couldn't get out of the way. He stood there, hopeless, his feet planted to the floor, his eyes glued to an expiring hourglass. It cut deep, shredding his insides.

Beep. Beep. Beep . . .

He pondered his turmoil, wondering which he feared most—losing his father or being alone in the world. Both were inevitable. Neither could be stopped or slowed down. All he could do now was brace for impact.

Beep. Beep. Beep . . .

Chapter 13

Deep bass sounds pounded the parking lot, vibrating car windows. Drew was parked, blanketed in darkness—aside from the glow of his phone—waiting to meet Neil at The Gentleman's Choice, a strip club not far from Palmer Heights.

Nearly two weeks had passed since Drew last went out with Neil, and they were overdue for a get-together. Neil, of course, had chosen the venue.

Between loitering in the parking lot after hours with Kara, then heading home to shower and change, Drew hadn't had a chance to drop by Mercy Vale Hospital after work. He dialed his father and raised the phone to his ear.

Voicemail.

"Hi Dad, it's Drew. Listen, I'm sorry I didn't get to come by tonight after work. Give me a shout if you get a chance. I'd love to hear how you're doing." He ended call, making a mental note to stay longer on his next visit.

Drew now had four training days under his belt. He found himself enjoying it, strangely enough—more specifically, enjoying his daily flirtatious interactions with Kara. More than once, Drew had returned to his seat in the training room to find a handwritten note folded on his chair, always signed with a hand-drawn heart.

Let's get drunk and play Twister, one of them had read.

Do you sleep naked? Because I do, read another.

But the most recent note had contained just ten characters—the digits of her phone number.

Little did Kara know that Drew had already covertly obtained her contact details on their first day working together. The sign-in sheet was left out in the open, after all.

Not wanting to come on too strong—charming a beautiful woman was foreign territory—he had stored it in his contacts for retrieval at a more appropriate time. But her latest note served as nothing if not an invitation. He selected Kara from his contacts and tapped out a simple greeting.

Drew: *Hi it's Drew*

A steady flow of male patrons lumbered in and out of The Gentleman's Choice. It wasn't a club known for the unprecedented sex appeal of its dancers. Roxie's, which was just a short mile down the road, recruited most of the top shelf talent in town. But The Gentleman's Choice was regarded for its moral and legal flexibility, offering a complete catalog of services—an open menu of fixed-price fantasies on demand. It was as much an underground brothel as a nudie bar.

The tired sign out front was trimmed with burned out and shattered light bulbs, but the club had no need for frivolities. Roadside advertising wasn't needed to draw in willing regulars.

It was nearly ten o'clock and Drew's phone vibrated.

Kara: *Hi Drew Thomson. Thought I'd never hear from you*

Drew: *How's it going?*

Kara: *Good. You creeping me on Facebook again? ;)*

Drew: *LOL No. Out with a friend*

Kara: *Then how come you're texting me?*

Drew hesitated before responding. Kara was gorgeous and fun, no doubt about it. And the attention she lavished on him was good for his ego. But she was just another pretty face—so why couldn't he stop thinking about her?

Drew: *I was thinking about you*

Kara: *Aww <3 You're not sick of me yet??*

Her comment reminded Drew of the time he had overheard one of Heather's friends—the queen bee of the Indiscreet Elite—complaining that men didn't hit on her in public. "It's just awful," she had said. "When you're this hot, guys are intimidated. They won't even approach me. I always have to make the first move and it feels slutty." Drew had cracked up. First, this particular female wasn't the catch she proclaimed herself to be. But even if she were, it was tough to pity the poor lonely hot girl.

Still, Drew had to wonder. He hadn't seen anyone in his training group—male or female—utter so much as a word to Kara. Not even Grease Monkey or Super Mario, who had made a sport out of trailing Bubbles around the premises, groping her every chance they got. Not that she seemed to mind. Was it possible that Kara lived in invisible anonymity, much as he did?

A loading wheel spun on his phone, signifying an incoming image download. A second later, a selfie of Kara populated his screen. She was standing in front of a full-length mirror, holding two different dresses against her body. He spotted her bare skin between them, giving away that she was stripped down to her bra and panties underneath. *What a tease.*

Kara: *Which one should I wear tomorrow?*

Drew: *Left*

Kara: *Thx*

Kara: *What are you and your friend up to?*

Drew: *Meeting for drinks*

Kara: *You're at a strip joint, aren't you*

Drew: *How'd you know?*

Kara: *Because boys are gross*

Drew: *You don't mean that*

Kara: *Ok, ok. You're not so bad but the rest are gross ;)*

Kara: *If I took off my clothes would you come drink with me*

Drew: *Yes. What's your address*

Kara: *LOL not tonight*

Drew: *Tomorrow night?*

Kara: *Ask me tomorrow night*

Drew's phone vibrated. An incoming text message from—Heather?

Heather: *You didn't tell me your dad has cancer*

Drew: *Guess it slipped my mind*

Heather: *I had to find out from Logan!!*

Drew: *Not surprised. He's got a big mouth*

Heather: *I'm going to go see him*

Drew: *K bye*

He probably should have reached out to Heather to tell her about his father's diagnosis. Russell was fond of Heather, and she had grown attached to the idea of being the daughter he never had. At the same time, Drew wanted to avoid giving her false hope, let alone one more reason to loiter in his life.

The thought that just six short weeks before he had been living with Heather left Drew suddenly unsettled. He and Heather had shared half a decade of history. She had never overtly pressured him to make life changes, nor to think toward the future. But they had had an unspoken under-standing that a forever after was the probable outcome, mostly because it followed the path of least resistance. In time, the thought of a forever after—of *anything* beyond the here and now, for that matter—had finally pushed Drew over the edge. In retrospect, Drew could only think of his time spent with Heather as a waste.

The here and now was Kara. She somehow reminded him to enjoy the moment and not worry about the future—because in the end, tomorrow never comes. She made him feel adequate, unflawed and without reason to change. As though he weren't an alcoholic, an addict, a gambling fiend, or a broken head case littered among the trash of Palmer Heights. He craved her body, of course, but more than anything, he craved the acceptance she dispensed—an alternative to the negative presumptions he believed about himself.

He swiped back to his chat with Kara.

Drew: *Send me a photo without holding up the dresses?*

Kara: *You're too much LOL*

Kara: *Don't you have naked ladies to look at over there*

Drew: *Maybe*

A new message from Neil.

Neil: *Bro where the fuck are you*

Drew: *Parking*

Neil: *Get your ass in here. There's pussy everywhere*

Back to Kara.

Drew: *I gotta go*

Kara: *Enjoy, you'll have to tell me all about it*

Drew: *I will*

Kara: *You're gonna drunk text me later aren't you*

Drew: *How do I know I'm not drunk texting you right now?*

Kara: *LOL see you tomorrow*

Drew slid his phone in his pocket and got out of the car.

* * *

The Gentleman's Choice was bursting at the seams.

Howls and cheers showered the main stage as a tall, lean dancer with faultless caramel skin got to her knees, doing away with her glittery top. She uncovered plump breasts, her ebony nipples standing firmly on end. She caressed each one in turn, rocking her hips to the thunderous music.

The song ended and the disc jockey began speaking. His deep voice sent shockwaves through listeners, almost loud enough to hurt Drew's ears. "Gentlemen, put your fucking hands together and make some noise for Jasmine." His voice had the cadence of an auctioneer, the sultry bass tones of a radio personality. A few men clapped perfunctorily. "Jasmine will be here all night to make your wildest dreams come true, gentlemen. But remember, money talks and bull-shit walks. So if you like what you see, offer Jasmine a gen-erous tip and she'll be sure to give you a special thank you."

Drew joined Neil who had chosen seats in front of the main stage. Even in this house of ill repute, Neil remained steadfast about his exterior, sporting designer threads and expensive cologne. He acknowledged Drew but remained silent, allowing the DJ to finish his public address.

" . . . and don't even think of going anywhere, because every hour on the hour tonight, three sexy ladies will be taking the main stage at once. I'll let you do the math, gen-tlemen—anything could happen. All for your viewing pleas-ure, and all part of Thirsty Thursdays here at The Gentleman's Choice." The next song began. " . . . I'm DJ Dan and it's about to get hot, hot, hot in here, gentlemen. Time to put your hands together again for Jasmine, returning to the main stage right now."

Each dancer got two songs on the main stage, as Drew recalled from the odd previous visit with Neil—a tease for the first song, then full nudity for the second. Jasmine walked back on stage, bent over, and gently slid her thong to the side.

"I've been here an hour, bro. What took you so long?"

"I was on the phone," Drew replied. "Seats in pervert's row, huh? Nice."

Neil winked.

"I meant to ask, how did things go with Becca?"

"Who the hell is Becca?"

"You know, the girl from The Stone Goblin."

Neil scanned his memory without success. "Doesn't ring a bell."

"She brought us drinks—she worked there. Young, wore a kilt, tan skin, big bouncy boobs." Drew had to holler to be heard over the music.

"Did I fuck her?"

"Yeah, probably. I mean, you left with her."

"Then obviously she had big boobs. Doesn't help."

Drew gave up. He wondered what it was like to entertain such a regular stream of busty females that each one could be so easily forgotten. It seemed jarring in contrast to the way that Kara consumed his mental resources.

Neil pulled out a wad of cash, rifling through it for a twenty-dollar bill. He inched toward the stage, presenting his gift to Jasmine. She crawled to him on all fours, arching her back for viewers on the sidelines. Taking Neil by the head, she pulled his face toward her chest, encouraging him to motorboat her naked breasts. She released her grip after a moment, offering him a suggestive wave of her hand and a blown kiss.

He settled back in next to Drew. "You want a turn?" He waved his fistful of cash.

As with most situations, Drew gravitated toward the role of silent observer rather than active participant. He was satisfied to take in the exhibition without experiencing it firsthand. "I'm good for now."

Drew felt something graze the back of his chair. He turned his head and saw two glamorous beauties—half-naked brunettes in clear heels—leading a dark-suited man in his fifties behind a plain black curtain. He had, no doubt, prepaid for a chunk of their time.

Neil perked up, as if he recalled something important. "Bro, you missed it. Before you got here, they had three chicks on stage at once, touching each other."

Drew recalled DJ Dan broadcasting a similar message. "You don't say?"

"Yeah, I recognized one of them, actually. She was eating the other two out. Got a hummer from her here last month."

"What did that cost you?"

"Like three hundred bucks." Neil paused, at first pensive then decidedly incensed. "Bro, are you my fucking accountant now? What the fuck is wrong with you?"

"Nothing is wrong with me."

"Did you start playing for the other team or something?"

"What? No."

"It's like you're always living in your head." Neil shouted, not just to be heard over the music, but to drive his point home. "You've been here five minutes now and I haven't seen you gawk at a single pair of tits yet. Relax and appreciate your surroundings a little."

"Got other stuff on my mind, I guess."

A woman in her early thirties in a taut black skirt approached them. She had a slender frame, wide eyes, heavily rouged cheeks, and full lips. Her white blouse was buttoned to her neck. She focused on Neil—likely to be the better tipper, but also the obvious alpha male—and asked, "What can I get for you?"

"Let me ask you a question first," Neil said. "How come you're the only one here with clothes on?"

Blouse smiled graciously, as if it were the first time someone had asked her that. "Policy. I'm not allowed to take attention away from the dancers."

Neil produced another twenty dollars. "But you've already got my attention."

Drew knew this interaction wouldn't go far. Sure, in any other setting, Blouse was a total knockout. But by contrast to the pounds of available bare flesh in the room, she surely wasn't Neil's top pick. But Neil had always enjoyed the thrill of the chase, to see how far his charisma—and wallet—could take him.

"Thanks," Blouse said, accepting his donation. "But really, I'll get into trouble if I show anymore skin."

Neil laughed. "Just a little skin. C'mon, bend the rules a bit. Undo your top a little for me."

Blouse glanced over her shoulder. The song was ending and DJ Dan was bellowing hurried streams of gibberish. It served as a brief distraction, so she surrendered. She unfastened the top few buttons of her blouse just far enough to show cleavage.

"That's better," Neil said.

Blouse closed her top and shook her head. "For twenty dollars, you could have had your pick of girls for one song. You could have touched her, too."

"But I wanted you." Neil gave her a wink.

Blouse made eye contact with Drew. "Your friend here is crazy."

"Tell me about it." But the music drowned him out. A new woman had taken the stage. She had short, spiky red hair, a nose ring, and thick tattooed thighs. She twirled around the pole with unexpected poise, still fully, albeit sparsely, dressed.

"Anyway," Blouse continued, "what'll you have?"

Neil squinted at Drew, and then turned back to her without consulting him. "Bring us each a single-malt scotch, neat."

She laughed. "You've got to be kidding me."

"What's so funny?"

"You're at The Gentleman's Choice, honey. Not The Playboy Mansion. We've got Bud or Bud Light—it's up to you."

Neil shook his head. "What kind of gentleman drinks Budweiser?"

Drew leaned in to be heard over the music. "Two tall cans of Bud will be fine, miss. Thank you."

Neil rolled his eyes.

"We always gets cans of Bud here," Drew explained. "You're thinking of Roxie's."

"Nah, bro. They used to stock better shit here."

No, they didn't. But when you visit so many of these places, it must be tough to keep track.

Spiky moved on to her second song. She alternated between bending over—gripping the pole between two firm, plentiful cheeks, and then sinking to the floor, suspending herself backward from the pole.

That metal pole has to be cold on her junk. Not to mention covered in germs.

"You must be chasing some serious tail these days," Neil commented.

"Not exactly."

"I mean, I haven't heard from you since—what? That day you dropped by my place to score some coke, I think."

"Well, there is this one chick—"

"My nigga." Neil tossed up a congratulatory hand.

"We're white. Stop it."

"I don't give a fuck. High five me."

Drew obeyed. "Anyway, she's, uh—" He had plenty to say about Kara. But choosing his words in such a way that

Neil would grasp them seemed unlikely.

"She works with you at the call center?"

"Yeah."

Neil began to slowly nod his head. "Ah, I get it. Say no more."

"What do you get exactly?"

"Saggy tits, stretch marks, tramp stamp, eight kids, food stamps. I get it. Enough to make any man's penis soft."

"Dickhead, no. She's stunning."

Neil rubbed his fingers together, the universal sign for money. "If she's such a top shelf piece of ass, how come she's working with you instead of trapping herself a sugar daddy?"

"She's, uh, the independent type, I guess."

"A feminist?"

"I didn't say that."

"You didn't have to. You fuck her yet?"

"No."

"You're out of practice, bro," Neil mused. "Spent too long shacked up with that horse-faced broad. Hillary or Heather or whatever her goddamn name was. But if this new chick lets you stick it in, mark my words. She'll have a thick fucking rug on her cunt and hairy armpits, too. These feminist bitches are all the same, bro. Fucking fat, disgusting, and bushy. You'll see."

Blouse returned with two cans of beer. Drew reached for his wallet, but Neil stopped him, keen to show off his spending power again. After she left, Neil turned his head toward the back of the club, and then tapped Drew on the shoulder. "Now's our chance."

"For what?"

"Now. Let's go." He led Drew to the bathroom. An empty stool was positioned by the door and assorted toiletries arranged in baskets spanned the counter next to the sinks. "The dude who sits in here normally—you know, the guy who washes your hands for tips? He's a smoker and I saw him dart out back. He's been going out every half hour or so."

"So?"

"So we've got five minutes." He opened each stall, confirming they were alone. "Come here." He gestured for Drew to enter the handicapped stall with him. "Brought us a little something."

Neil closed the door behind them, and removed a plastic baggie from his jacket pocket. He shook a small heap of white powder on the back of the toilet and deftly cut it into two fine lines with his bank card. He pulled out a dollar bill and rolled it into a narrow tube. He lowered his face to the tank, and ripped the first line. He pinched his nose and then ran his finger across the tank and massaged the leftover powder onto his gums. Drew took the dollar bill and did the same. The blow instantly rushed to his head and livened his pulse, awakening his senses. They pocketed a few breath mints near the sink and walked back to their seats.

"Thanks for that," Drew said.

"My pleasure, bro. It's a good night to celebrate."

"What are we celebrating?"

"I got promoted to division manager at work."

That could've been me. "Congrats. But I thought you were thinking of leaving?"

"Nah, bro. Things got better since you left. They gave me a nice bump in salary. Plus I got my own sexy assistant. Boned her twice al—"

"All in a week or two, huh?"

"All in a week, bro. You know I don't fuck around."

Define 'fuck around.'

"And I'm moving into a new condo on the first."

"That's next week."

"Yes, it is."

"You really don't fuck around. What was wrong with the old condo?"

"New one's bigger."

"And bigger is better, I guess."

"That's what she said." Neil laughed at his own worn out quip. He eyed the full can of beer in front of him with disdain then surrendered, raising it in the air. "Cheers, my friend."

Drew lifted his can.

"I'll be having a housewarming party. I trust you'll be there."

Drew thought of his father, who was likely passed out in his hospital bed at the moment, savoring the sweet serenity of a drug induced coma. It occurred to Drew that he had been at The Gentleman's Choice with Neil for almost an hour—nearly enough time for the next trio of ladies to hit the stage—and his father's condition hadn't come up even once. "I'll try to make it." He paused. "It's just that I won't be able to if—"

"Holy shit!" A new dancer strutted on stage. "Look at the tits on that bitch. Jesus Christ."

Drew shrugged. "Yeah, look at them."

Chapter 14

Kara scrunched her face, her chest full of smoke. She'd just put the joint to her lips and taken an enormous drag, drawing it to the depths of her lungs. She was reeling, dizzy, as though her next trick would be to pass out.

"Are you okay?" Drew asked, chuckling. They were standing behind the Transtel building, sandwiched between a couple of dumpsters and a dormant security vehicle.

She exhaled at long last, dispersing a thick haze. "Yeah, I'm doing just fine."

"This bud Marcus sells isn't half bad, is it?"

"Who's Marcus?"

"He's my new dealer." Drew carefully removed the burning joint from Kara's fingers and took a puff. "Full-time student, part-time dealer, covert tutor, and just another friendly face in the neighborhood. I give him a call and he drops by my place with whatever I need."

"Service with a smile." She tittered, her eyes red and glazed over, and then broke out in uncontrollable laughter.

"You really do get the giggles when you smoke, huh?"

"Oh God, this is embarrassing," she cackled.

"Nothing to be embarrassed about." He watched her with amusement. "But while we're on the topic, do you know any good dirty jokes?"

She shook her head, unable to concentrate. "Do you,

Drew Thomson?"

"Yeah, I got one."

Kara bobbed her head up and down, urging him to tell it.

"A man says to his wife, 'Let's try something kinky. To-night I'm going to come in your ear.' "

She keeled over, her face bright red, nearing purple, as if Drew had already delivered the punch line.

"The wife was shocked. 'You can't do that. It might make me go deaf,' she said."

"He wants to nut in her ear!" Kara gasped for air. "Oh my God . . . "

Drew took another drag, delaying the rest of the joke for effect. Kara was, after all, already in stitches. He opened his mouth a crack, letting smoke trickle past his dry lips. "So the husband says, 'I've been shooting my load in your mouth for ten years now, and it hasn't shut you up yet.' "

Kara was unable to move or speak. She vibrated in place like a Tickle Me Elmo.

She's probably had enough. Drew took one final hit, the joint burned to its crutch, then tossed what was left.

A few seconds later—or perhaps several minutes—Kara was gradually regaining control of herself, wiping tears of laughter from her eyes. "Oh shit! That was too good."

"Glad you liked that one."

"I've got one."

"Is it dirty?"

She grinned. "Why did God invent women?" Kara looked eager to blurt out the rest.

"Why?"

"To carry semen from the bedroom to the bathroom."

Drew doubled up in delight, speechless at her unexpected lewdness, and higher than even he had realized. Sure, he found the joke tasteless and hilarious in equal measure, but he also enjoyed hearing Kara say the word semen. "I'm glad we did this."

Kara looked unstable. She toppled against Drew, uncoordinated, planting a sloppy kiss on his cheek. He was slow to respond, unsure what to do. "Thanks," he said after a moment.

"I like you, Drew Thomson." Her speech was hollow and distant.

He nodded. "I, uh, like you, too."

Kiss her back.

But the moment expired, each waning second lessening the impact of any possible reaction. He lost his nerve, eventually asking, "Are you hungry?"

"I'm starving."

"Want to hit up the cafeteria? Maybe they're serving those heat lamp French fries we all know and love."

She steadied a shaking hand on his arm. "Sounds good. Lead the way."

They walked to the front of the building, mere hours from finishing their week of training.

Chapter 15

"Oh, believe me, I understand. That must have been so embarrassing for you." Drew worked to placate a disgruntled caller. He slouched in his chair, cupping his head in his hand, broadcasting artificial empathy through his headset.

He glanced over at Kara, who was watching him from two workstations over. It was Monday, their first day on the job, and new calls were coming in slowly. So far, Drew had managed to handle all of them without effort or incident. "Yes, I have two kids myself," he explained. "I know if either of my daughters witnessed my card declining at Target, I'd be upset, too."

Their training group had been divided that morning. Numerous businesses outsourced their customer service initiatives to Transtel, which meant that trainees were needed on a variety of campaigns. And those predicted to perform at the highest levels were assigned to their largest—and most lucrative—corporate clients.

No matter what campaign a team member worked on, the job was self-explanatory. Follow the script on the computer, then—depending what the customer said—choose from a list of concerns at the bottom of the screen. Click whatever option most closely matched the caller's problem, and move on to another screen filled with robotic jargon-filled prompts.

Drew, Kara, and Bubbles had all been assigned to receive calls for a certain credit card company, notorious for awarding high credit limits to unworthy recipients. They were frontline customer service agents for cardholders, granted access to billing details, and able to perform simple tasks, such as setting travel notifications. But for anything more complicated—fraud, credit limit increases, and reward programs, for example—it was their job to escalate the call to an offsite department.

Drew was overjoyed. As far as he was concerned, his only job was to convince each caller that he or she needed to speak to someone else. It was like getting paid to shirk responsibility.

He continued to diffuse his caller. "Yes, ma'am. You are so right. And you know what, I don't normally do this, but I'm going to connect you with our VIP support team. They have all sorts of powers I don't. If anyone can make this right, it's them. They might even be able to compensate you for your hardships. Let me transfer you there right now."

Kara smirked. "VIP support, huh?"

"It worked," Drew replied. "Fucking child's play." He took three big swallows from his treasured water bottle, savoring the burn that accompanied each one.

Hungry Paul paced around the corner. He had been darting between his newest team members all day—remarkably quick for his size—offering assistance where it was needed. "Nice job, Drew."

"Thanks, Paul."

"Yeah, I overheard most of that last call. You're great with people."

"I try."

"But you can't lie."

"Lie?" Drew donned his best look of perplexity.

"Yeah. VIP support lines and that kind of thing. Even talking about your kids—"

"They don't know if I have kids."

"Do you?"

"None that I know of."

"The problem arises when they call back—and believe me, they always call back. If they get you again, are you going to remember everything you told them?"

Thinking that far into the future made Drew's head hurt. "Probably not."

"Exactly. Always tell the truth and you won't need a good memory. Got it?"

"Got it."

Hungry Paul walked away.

"You're on fire," Kara said. She eyed Drew's water bottle. "That isn't filled with some sort of happy juice, is it?"

"Maybe."

"Feel like sharing?" She bolted upright.

Drew recognized what was happening. A loud beep had rung in her ear, signifying the arrival of her next caller. That same beep had startled him more than once that day.

Kara spun around in her seat, jabbing at the cumbersome digital display on her desk. She attempted to unmute her headset but it looked like she was having trouble. "Oh shit. I think I just hung up on someone."

Drew laughed. "At least you didn't lie to them."

She scrunched her face at him. It reminded him of how she looked when she was high.

Beep. A new caller. *That's what I get for laughing at her.* Drew answered the phone with all the cheer he could muster. He prompted the caller for personal information—part of the mandatory security check—entering her responses on his computer. All at once, Kara's unmistakable scent filled his nostrils. She passed behind him, dropping a folded piece of paper on his desk.

"Uh, hang on one sec." Drew placed the call on hold and unfolded the note.

Follow me, it read with a small heart underneath.

Drew returned to his caller. "Uh, ma'am, I'm so sorry, but I'm going to have to give you a call back. There's been a fire alarm in the building and I'm told we have to evacuate." He ended the call, dropped himself out of queue, and followed Kara around the corner with his water bottle in hand.

She was a few paces down a nearby hallway, standing at the door to the nearest women's restroom. She beckoned for him to follow before going inside.

Drew looked around with trepidation. He took another swig of vodka, marched to the door, and entered the bathroom behind her.

It was empty.

He was headed toward the stalls when Kara reached out and grabbed him by the collar, pulling him inside the one closest to the entrance. She shut the door, locked it, and grabbed his water bottle, placing it on the toilet behind her.

"Kara—"

She silenced him by pressing her mouth against his, knocking him backward against the closed door. Her fingers locked between his and she guided his hand down the front of her dress, cradling it around a tender breast. He clasped her warm flesh as she ran her hands through his hair, swirling her tongue around his, their breathing heavy. She nibbled his lower lip, tugging it into her mouth. Drew slid his free hand down the outside of her dress. He traced her figure with his palm, teasing her slender waist. She extended a hand downward, stroking him dutifully. She took a step backward and dropped to her knees on the tiled floor. Her hand on his belly, she silently directed him to remain propped against the door. Belt, button, zipper—she ripped his pants down in one fierce motion.

"Are you, uh—"

Kara looked up at him, her intense green eyes overwhelming his senses. She placed a slender hand around his shaft, gripping it ardently, and brought her other hand to her lips, motioning for him to hush. She wrapped her mouth around him, and Drew whimpered with pleasure. Her mouth moved back and forth, slobbering and slurping, droplets of her warm saliva pooling on his skin. *I can't believe this is happening.* Drew wavered between closing his eyes and watching Kara, not wanting to miss an instant of her frenzied performance.

The bathroom door opened and Drew heard two women enter. It sounded as though their footsteps stopped in front of the mirror.

The first woman spoke. "So I told the dumb bitch I couldn't do anything for her. Like, if she lost her credit card, it's her own fault, right?"

Bubbles.

"Yeah," the second woman said. "I've already had to escalate three calls to Paul today."

Drew didn't recognize the second voice.

Kara signaled for Drew to remain silent.

" . . . if you ask me, this place is a fucking joke. I hate it here," Bubbles said.

"Today's only our first day on the phones. It'll probably get better."

"I doubt that, especially since . . . "

Drew tried to tune it out. *Oh fuck, I'm gonna come . . .*

Drew motioned to Kara that he was about to finish, thinking she might prefer to remove him from her mouth.

114

But she held him between her moist lips, raising her eyes to meet his, her expression saying, *Do it! I'm ready.*

" . . . so I guess I'll stick it out for now," Bubbles whined.

"That's probably the smartest thing."

Drew's face contorted in pleasurable stupor, his toes wiggling as he arched his back, gasping. He shook with elation, rattling the stall door.

Bubbles and her friend fell silent. "Oh God, I think someone's getting head in there," he heard Bubbles say. She had likely noticed his feet and her knees below the stall.

"Gross," the other woman said. "Let's get out of here."

Kara freed Drew from her mouth at last, beaming, pleased with herself. He panted, speechless, sweat on his brow.

"What—what did I do to deserve that?"

"Don't mention it, Drew Thomson." Kara stood and leaned in to kiss him but stopped short, laughing. "I'm kidding. I know you don't want me to kiss you after giving you a blowjob."

"Maybe just take a drink first," he teased.

"Good idea." Kara picked up the water bottle and took several swallows. She held the last one in her mouth and swished it around. She kissed Drew on the lips, her hand resting on his stubbly cheek.

Drew was torn—grateful for this unexpected miracle, but wanting more. He kissed her back and slid a hand under her dress, allowing his fingers to wander in search of her panties, intending to pull them down, but discovering bare flesh instead.

"I told you," she said. "I don't wear underwear, at least not if I don't have to." She pulled his hand from under her dress and held it against her chest. "We've both been out of queue for over ten minutes. Paul's going to start asking questions."

Drew frowned. "When can we, uh, do this again?"

She gave Drew a spirited shove. "That's the problem with boys. You give them a little, and it's all they think about."

"Are you free one night this week?"

Kara thought for a moment. "Yes, one night this week, I'll be all yours. Promise." She hesitated. "Are you going to take me on a date first?"

"Uh, sure—I can do that."

"I'm kidding, Drew Thomson." She laughed again. "How about I just come spend the night at your place? We'd have more fun, I think."

You're going to beg me for the name of my interior decorator. "That would be great. Just be sure to forget your pajamas."

"I already told you I sleep naked, Drew Thomson." Kara rolled her eyes. "It's like you don't even read the notes I pass you." She winked and unlocked the stall door. "I'm going to head back before we both get fired."

Drew nodded and watched her leave the restroom. She was holding his treasured water bottle captive, but as far as he was concerned, she could keep it.

Chapter 16

A familiar face emerged from the elevator, one that hospital staff had grown accustomed to seeing on the fifth floor. "Hello there, Drew," a woman in scrubs called from the nurses' station. He couldn't recall her name, but she was large, jovial, and had a Caribbean accent. Her liveliness seemed dissonant with the bleak energy of the cancer ward. "How was work today?"

Would it be inappropriate to tell her I got my dick sucked at work? "Oh, all right, I guess. Same as always."

"That's good," she said. "I bet your dad will be happy to see you."

If he's awake.

Drew could have walked the convoluted route to his father's room blindfolded. But he kept his eyes wide open, unable to ignore the wretchedness around him. A number of the patients changed on every visit. Some, who he had noted days prior, would be missing, having checked out one way or another. And new arrivals would be settling in around every corner. It was like playing Russian roulette with cancer instead of a gun.

As he approached his father's room, Holly emerged, halting her rapid pace to greet him. She offered him the same insincere smile as always. "Nice to see you."

Is it? Because it would be a lot nicer if Dad wasn't here. "It's nice to see you, too," he replied. "How's Dad?"

Holly's face hardened. "He's hanging in there."

"How much—"

"He might not have a lot of time left, I'm afraid." She frowned, folding her arms. "He's a wonderful man. Keeps everyone here in stitches."

"I can imagine," Drew said, but he couldn't.

"So just make the most of the time you have with him, okay?"

He gave her a subtle nod.

"Well, go on in and say hello. He was awake earlier, but he's napping now." She started walking away, adding, "It's so great that you and your brother came to see him at the same time."

Wonderful news.

Logan was bent over the bedrail, watching their father sleep. The privacy curtain was again closed around Patrick who, in all likelihood, was every bit as unconscious as Russell.

Drew plodded forward, taking the spot next to Logan. He observed their father's condition—it appeared no better or worse than on his last visit.

"Andrew."

"Logan." Drew glanced at his brother from the corner of his eye. "How's your face?"

"It's fine, thank you."

"You actually found time in your busy schedule for a visit, huh?"

"I've visited Russell a few times. We must show up at different times of the day." A silent standoff endured between them for a moment, Logan surrendering first. "How long have you known?"

"Known what?"

"You called me a faggot at the cemetery. Second time this year."

"Yeah, so?"

Logan slowed his speech, putting emphasis on each word. "So how long have you known?"

Drew felt like a toddler trying to make sense of counting. "You're gay?"

Logan turned his head toward Drew. "Don't act so surprised."

But he was surprised. "I think I should be asking you the same thing. How long have you known?"

Logan diverted his eyes to the far end of the room, calculating his response. "Since I was sixteen or so. Thereabouts."

Drew shot Logan a look of contempt, uncertain how he had spent the last ten years in the dark. "Why didn't you tell me before now?"

Logan took a deep breath and curled his lower lip, indecisive. "When I—I officially came out, the kids at school weren't exactly kind about it. Most of them had already made up their minds about me—"

"I had already graduated by then."

"That's right. You weren't there." Another deep breath. "I came home one day and told Russell, and he gave me two choices. I could either take it back, which I knew I couldn't, or I could stop living under his roof." Logan's words came out slow, intentional, and distressed.

Drew blinked. "That's bullshit. You left Dad—that's on you, not him."

"I wish that were true, Andrew." It was Logan's turn to blink, as if lost in painful memory. "If I had abandoned Russell, as you say I did, I would at least have the chance to apologize to him now. You know, before it's too late." Logan's eyes filled with moist regret. "Instead, I get to watch him die, knowing he didn't want me for a son."

Drew wanted to lash out, to tear Logan to pieces. To make him eat his words. He couldn't accept what he was hearing. But on some level, he knew Logan was telling the truth—even if he wasn't ready to admit it out loud.

"I think Mom knew. We were young when she died, of course. Just kids back then. But I remember her telling me that she loved me no matter what . . . " A tear spilled down Logan's cheek. "Even if I was different from the other boys. Then she passed, and it never came up again. Not until I was a teenager."

Drew lowered his eyes to their father, fighting to comprehend the shifting paradigm before him. Russell's breathing was ragged, but he was otherwise blissful and sedated. Yet somehow he was a different man than just moments before. Drew felt a sudden surge of guilt. He and Logan had spent their adult years at odds, persistent tension between them. Had Russell been the original source of that tension? Then again, he was the man who had taught Drew to be complacent, amenable to whatever came next in life. How could he have shut out one of his sons?

"Dad never told me," Drew whispered.

"He was embarrassed, Andrew. He didn't want to believe it."

"You never told me."

"I—I couldn't. You wouldn't have understood."

What Drew was beginning to understand was that he and Logan were, in some ways, living a paralleled existence—both marred by the loss of their mother and stunted in life by their father. "I might have," he said. "But you didn't give me a chance. Why are you telling me this now?"

Logan brooded for a moment. "Russell's on his deathbed, Andrew. It's given me a lot to think about. And there's something else you should know."

"What?"

"You have a brother-in-law."

It took Drew a moment to translate what that meant. "You're *married*?"

"When I left home, I met Stephen."

"Stephen?" Drew had never met Stephen, but knew him by name. "I thought Stephen was your roommate."

"Yes, at first. He was a few years older than me. He took me in while I finished high school, and then college afterwards. But we've been together nine, almost ten years now. And we officially got married last year."

"You did?"

"Yes. Nothing flashy, despite what you might think about me. It was just the two of us at city hall, and it was exactly how we wanted it." Logan debated before adding, "You'd like him."

Drew glanced at Logan's left hand. "You don't wear a ring."

"I don't feel the need to draw attention to it. Last thing I need is strangers judging me. I mean, my own father couldn't accept me. Why should anybody else? I was about to start a career in law where image counts for everything. And besides, Stephen and I know the truth, that's all that matters. We don't need to broadcast it to anyone else."

"You even kept it a secret on Facebook." Drew was referencing Logan's relationship status. It was unlike him to omit any shred of his success online.

"It isn't a secret, Andrew. People only keep secrets if they think they've done something wrong. We just don't draw attention to our relationship. That's all."

Drew shook his head. "I'm sorry, Logan."

"You are?"

"Yeah, I am." Drew strained to feel empathy or compassion for his brother—a normal human response—but at best, he was only able to muster a faint sense of discomfort in the pit of his stomach. "But here's what I don't get. Why are you here? If Dad turned his back on you all those years ago, why do you care what happens to him now?"

"Because Russell's my father, whether I like it or not."

It occurred to Drew that his father wasn't a wealthy man, and that he hadn't seen a bill from the hospital. "Wait, are you paying for Dad's stay here?"

Logan nodded halfheartedly, changing the subject with haste. "I know you and Russell have always been close, Andrew. But have you considered how much he influences you? How passive he is about everything—as if nothing good ever comes from trying?"

Even if Drew agreed, he felt uncomfortable speaking ill of their father—especially since he was mere inches from them on his deathbed. "Maybe."

"Give it some thought. Your life doesn't have to go like his."

"Like his how, exactly?"

"Come on. I can smell weed on your clothes and booze on your breath."

Guilty as charged.

"Andrew. Jesus. Look, it's your life, and you can live it however you want. But Russell lived as a prisoner of his own design. You don't have to do the same thing. You still have time to change if you want to."

Drew was agitated, unable to process Logan's cautionary tale.

"I'm not trying to preach," Logan said. "I know I'm not perfect. But I want you to be happy, and—"

"I'm not sure I would know what happiness looks like

even if I woke up one day and found it staring me in the face."

Sure, getting high with Kara pleased him, at least for a few minutes. The thought of her body excited him, too. Even having a job that he could do drunk seemed worthy of celebration. But these were arbitrary moments in time, not permanent solutions. *Are fleeting moments of pleasure the same thing as happiness?*

Drew had a lot to think about—with any luck, a lot to accept. But he felt unsure of himself at that moment, insecure, as though he were seeing his father in a new light. A light that changed everything it touched. He had come to think of his father as a safety net of sorts. Someone who allowed him to be his true self. The one person who had no expectations for him. But now it seemed that being himself was only good enough if he promised never to change.

Logan laid a hand on Drew's shoulder. His unexpected contact caused Drew to flinch. "I'd still be happy to have lunch with you one day."

"Sure. I'll text you."

Logan acknowledged his response with a bow of his head.

Drew stepped into the hallway.

Heather was approaching from a short distance. "I wondered if I might find you here," she said.

"Did you know Logan's gay?"

Heather seemed to contemplate his question. "I had my suspicions. Why? He just told you?"

"Yeah."

"How do you feel about that?"

"Disappointed."

"How come?"

"Because he didn't tell me before now."

Heather pursed her lips, as though she were holding

something back. "To be fair, it's not like you ever made an effort to get to know him."

"I know. But maybe it isn't too late."

"Maybe." She ran her fingers through her hair. "Have you been doing okay otherwise?"

"Just peachy."

"Good. How's the new job going?"

"Yeah, listen, Heather—I've got to get going."

She winced, put off by his abrupt response. "All right, take care then."

"You too."

Chapter 17

The morning sun was rising over Northwood Park, illuminating the horizon with golden hues, extinguishing darkness from the lush landscape.

Drew awoke on a bench to the sound of birds chirping. He sat upright, clutching a brown paper bag in his hand, his body aching, his head pounding, his mouth dry. The sunlight in the distance burned his bloodshot eyes.

Before him was an elaborate paved trail, occupied by joggers, cyclists, and dog walkers—all performing their morning routines, paying Drew no mind. He was just another homeless drunk by the looks of it. The trail followed the edge of an expansive and tranquil pond, its cobalt surface still, disturbed only by the gentle ripples of ducks and geese.

He glanced at his phone. In less than two hours, he was due to arrive at work. But the thought of moving seemed intolerable. Returning to the hospital for his car, driving home to Palmer Heights to shower and change, and then getting to Transtel—he'd barely have time.

He sent a text message to Kara.

Drew: *Not going to make it in today. Feeling sick*

The clear morning sky stretched high above his head, promising the arrival of a perfect summer day—but all Drew could think about was sleeping off the compulsion to vomit. He leaned back, hoping for his stomach to settle and his head to stop spinning. *At least I found out how much I have to drink to achieve a hangover.* He took in the sounds of all the active people around him. *Fucking try-hards.*

"Dude, you're sleeping on my bench," said a stern female voice.

Drew reacted in slow motion, opening his eyes grievously, getting his bearings with pronounced difficulty. Before him stood a tall blonde woman with her hair in a ponytail. She was trim, obviously fit, in her late twenties, decked out in a track jacket and yoga pants worth more than his car. She looked serious—a hand on her hip, her mouth curled in a display of dissatisfaction. He met her stoic gaze. "Didn't know it was yours."

She unzipped her pocket and pulled out a Ziploc bag containing two slices of bread. "I feed the ducks on this bench every morning."

Drew turned to the center of the bench, pointing to a commemorative plaque. In Memory Of Angela Thomson, it read. "Looks like it belonged to my family first."

She gave the plaque a quick read. "Who's Angela Thomson?"

"My mom. Died twenty years ago in this exact spot."

"I'm sorry—"

"You didn't know. It's fine."

"I've never noticed that before, and I sit here almost every morning when I'm done jogging." She said it as though it was unlike her to ever miss a detail, no matter how minute. "I guess I've always been absorbed by the view."

This view was probably the last thing Mom ever saw.

Drew was unsure what to say, and striking up a conversation with a stranger was about the last thing he wanted to do.

She glanced at the paper bag in his hand. "Do you often

get drunk on your mom's bench at six in the morning?"

"There's a first time for everything." He held out the brown paper bag. "Why? You want a sip?"

She sat beside Drew, resting herself on the edge of the bench, her long legs stretched outward, the perspiration glistening on her skin. "No, thanks. I don't drink."

Barrel of fucking laughs, she is.

She looked beyond the pond at a row of trees in the distance. "I lost my mom, too. Almost fifteen years ago now."

Why do people share their stories with me? Isn't it obvious I don't give a shit? "That's too bad."

"I've come to terms with it." She stuck out her hand. "I'm Sierra Emery, by the way."

Drew ignored the gesture and chose not to reply.

"Should I just guess your name then?"

He sighed. "Go for it."

"Rumpelstiltskin? Rumpelstiltskin . . . Thomson?"

Is this bitch retarded? "It's Drew."

"Nice to meet you, Drew." Sierra opened her bag of bread and began tearing off pieces, tossing them in front of her feet, luring ducks and geese onto the path. The birds waddled to her, obstructing the trail for joggers and cyclists alike.

"You're gonna get one of those ducks squashed by a bike," Drew said.

"You think so?"

"Yeah, they're crossing the path to come eat."

"Hasn't happened yet, not in all the years I've been coming here."

"You've been coming here for years?"

Sierra gave him her version of a smile, making her look something like a lanky department store mannequin modeling athletic attire. "Something about this spot. I've been coming here every morning almost ever since I moved into this neighborhood."

"You must be my guardian angel."

Sierra snorted. "Hardly."

Drew lowered his eyes to the ground. "Believe it or not, this is actually the first time I've visited this bench since, well, since I was a kid, I guess."

"Oh. What brought you here today?" She appeared genuinely interested.

Assuming a spot on this bench had seemed like a great idea the night before, even if Drew couldn't explain why. It was as though this spot had called to him, drawing him in like a magnet. As if he were meant to be there. Although drinking himself into oblivion was his own idea—no divine intervention there. Still, he had expected to be left to his own devices—alone, in quiet, drunken isolation. Yet here he was, being interrogated by a complete stranger. A chance encounter he hadn't predicted and didn't appreciate. He would have preferred to start his day with a silent recovery period, an opportunity to allow his head to cease its violent spinning. To regain some semblance of balance and return home to his bare mattress, which, in comparison to the bench, sounded luxurious.

Sierra was still fixated on Drew, awaiting his response.

"Dad is in the hospital next door."

"Is it serious?"

"Yeah, he's going to die soon."

"Oh."

"I, uh, learned something new about him last night."

"Was it something important?"

"I guess so. Something I couldn't believe, really. The only way I could think to make sense of it was to come here and clear my head."

Sierra tossed her remaining crumbs to the birds. "But you didn't clear your head." She gestured toward the concealed bottle in his hand.

"This is how I clear my head."

Sierra looked doubtful. "Or maybe it's how you avoid confronting what's really going on in here." She tapped a finger on his chest.

"Are you a fucking Sadness Doctor or something?"

That's the first time I've ever said Sadness Doctor out loud and it sounds ridiculous.

"A sadness doctor?" Sierra scratched her head. "I'm not sure what that is, dude. I'm an accountant, actually."

"Shouldn't you be getting ready for work then?"

"I have the morning off."

Must be my lucky day.

"How about you?" she asked.

Drew replied, making no effort to hide his exasperation with her never-ending questions. "Yeah, same. I'm taking the morning off. The whole day, in fact."

"And what is it that you do?"

"Nothing interesting. I spent most of my twenties in sales, but now I work at a call center."

"I see."

"What do you see exactly?" he demanded.

"I see that you're in a lot of pain. You're lost and hurting and confused. Not that I'm judging you—we've all been there."

I doubt that. Drew had difficulty taking Sierra at face value. This persnickety upper middle class chick had appeared out of nowhere, making baseless assumptions, her commentary cloaked in passive aggressive rhetoric. As though she—the type who never missed a day of jogging—had the necessary life experiences to offer useful insights to others. The entire interaction reeked of self-righteousness. Sierra was, if nothing else, a suitable candidate for the Indiscreet Elite. A busybody know-it-all with a God complex, shilling meaningless advice to anyone who would listen.

"Maybe I just see some of my former self in you," she continued. "Just thought I might be able to relate, that's all—"

"You can't relate to shit. Do you make a habit of sitting down next to strangers in the park and psychoanalyzing them? Regurgitating whatever garbage you read in a Tony Robbins book?"

She looked more amused than offended. "No need for hostility, dude. Let's not take this out of context. I mean, do you make a habit of searching for answers at the bottom of a bottle, then passing out in public places?"

"None of your goddamn business."

"It isn't my business, I know. But you can't blame me for reaching out to someone who might need help."

Drew lifted his eyes, allowing them to roam the pond. The ducks and geese had returned to their habitat, now that Sierra was out of bread, gliding with grace from one spot to the next. None of them looked concerned for the future. Whether Sierra returned with bread or not, they would find food. They had a home, companionship, and they lived for the moment, liberated from the worry of what might happen next. *I should have been born a duck.*

"I'm sorry if I came on too strong," Sierra said at last. "Would you prefer if I left you alone?"

Drew contemplated her question. It seemed that every person in his life had a role to play, encouraging him to remain incomplete, strengthening his tendency to be complacent. Yet here was Sierra, extending her hand, offering her own unique brand of support. He decided that he had nothing to lose by hearing her out.

"No," he said, reluctant at first. "No, I don't want to be alone right now."

Sierra looked pleased, as though she had expected a different response. "All right. How about we continue this chat over coffee?"

"Sure. Sounds fine."

"I'm just going to jog home real quick, okay? I live just around the corner. I'll change out of these sweaty clothes and meet you back here in fifteen minutes—twenty tops."

"I won't move a muscle," he said. "You can count on it."

Sierra stood, stretching her long limbs and then sprinting into the eastern sunrise.

Drew stood for the first time in hours. His head screamed for mercy, thousands of invisible nails penetrating his temples. He tossed his brown paper bag in the trash next to the bench. *Does this chick devote her life to helping people, or is it something about me?* He sat down again and shut his eyes, awaiting Sierra's return.

Chapter 18

Drew walked alongside Sierra, matching her leisurely pace. She stood a couple inches taller than he did, close to six feet, mostly legs. With his head still throbbing, he appreciated the opportunity to move in smaller strides.

"Do you always invite bums on park benches out for coffee?"

"Only friendly looking bums." Her attempt at humor came across condescending more than anything else.

They arrived at her favorite café, and judging by its exterior, Drew felt certain he would stick out like a vagrant. Cool Beans was situated in a small, red brick building, its storefront signage barely visible. It was the epitome of snotty affluence. The interior of the café was aged, just old enough to be modern again—exposed brick, rustic wooden fixtures, and vintage adornments throughout. It felt cramped and chic all at once, the overhead droning of indie rock abrasive by conventional standards. Drew observed the décor and patrons alike. Young trendsetters—young even by his standards—gathered at tables, others working alone in front of MacBooks. They were oddly matched, androgynous, wearing plaid tops and distressed jeans, as though this crowd had coordinated their outfits online.

Drew and Sierra stood in line to order. Drew's phone vibrated in his pocket.

Kara: *Sorry to hear you're sick! Maybe I gave your penis germs :)*
Drew: *You gave my penis exactly what it needed*
Kara: *I'm looking forward to seeing more of it*
Kara: *But I guess tonight is no good? :(*

Had she asked him yesterday, when they were alone in the restroom stall, he would have said that tonight was perfect. But recovering from a debilitating hangover, he felt delaying their sex date was his only reasonable option.

Drew: *How about tomorrow?*
Kara: *Tomorrow works :)*

"Is that your girlfriend you're texting?" Sierra asked.

"Why would you think that?"

She shrugged. "You seem involved in the conversation, and you're smiling for the first time since I met you. I figured it must be a girl."

"She's, uh, not exactly my girlfriend."

"Not exactly?" She was intrigued. "But you are having sex with her, right?"

Drew didn't know how to take that. "No, for your information. Not yet—but soon, I hope."

"Uh huh."

They inched forward in line.

"Do you love her?"

"I—I don't think so, although I'd like to."

"What does that mean?"

"I, uh, don't know how to love someone."

"Does she love you?"

"I have no idea."

Sierra scanned the chalkboard menu. "I've had a lot of sex," she said, nonchalant.

Drew scrambled to invent a follow-up question, but it was their turn to order. Drew stared at the barista behind the counter. He sported shaggy, jet black hair with side-swept bangs and more eyeliner than most women.

"I'll have a nonfat green tea latte," Sierra said.

"Got it," Hipster said. He shifted his focus to Drew with a hint of disapproval. "And you?"

"Can I just have just a regular coffee with some sugar?"

Hipster gave his head a subtle shake, disgusted at the thought of such a mainstream order. He took their cash and got to work.

Sierra and Drew shuffled to the opposite end of the counter to wait for their beverages. "You've had a lot of sex, huh?" he asked.

"Yeah, dude." She chuckled, lowering her voice a little. "For years—in college and for a few years after that. I was open to trying just about anything."

Drew hadn't thought of her in a sexual context before that moment. Sierra was attractive, no doubt. She had deep blue eyes, milky skin, prominent cheekbones, and a distinguished jawline that gave her face the shape of a cover model. A pretty girl—Eastern European, perhaps—but certainly no match for Kara, and doused in just enough melancholy to make her appear aloof.

"I'm surprised. You seem . . . " Drew inspected her change of attire. She looked like a kindergarten teacher dressed in billowy slacks, a blouse that covered the full length of her arms, and sensible flats, " . . . a bit conservative."

"Now I am, sure. But I had an experimental phase. I tried to find love wherever I could, however I could, and the truth is, I had a lot of fun doing it. But it wasn't fulfilling. It was just *fucking*. A means to draw my self-worth from others."

That made no sense to Drew. If he had women lining up at his door, he'd feel plenty fulfilled. *Probably the way Neil feels all the time.*

Hipster handed them their drinks. They chose a private table in the corner, a chair on either side.

"My point is," Sierra continued, "this girl—"

"Kara."

"Kara, sure. Just be careful what you wish for. Not all that glitters is gold." She took a shallow sip from her steaming mug. "So you're a sales guy?"

"Used to be. I worked in corporate sales for a little over three years."

"You don't seem like a sales guy."

"How do you mean?"

She considered her response before speaking. "You seem a bit disinterested in people, that's all. And sales guys usually have a certain way of conversing with others. As if they're always trying to get people to like them."

He gave her a flippant wave of his hand. "It was a job and I was good at it. That's all."

"Did you enjoy it?"

"Oh, God no, not at all. You're right—I'm not a people person."

"That's what I mean. But you're good at adapting to different situations, right?"

I'm here talking to you, aren't I? "I guess so."

"What happened to your mom?" Sierra asked. "You said she died where that bench was built, but you didn't say how."

Her persistent questioning reminded Drew of the first conversation he had had with Kara in the Transtel cafeteria. "She was murdered."

"That's tragic." She frowned, tilting her head to the side. "You never got to say goodbye."

"I was eight at the time."

"And now your father's on his deathbed?"

"Lung cancer. Smoked three packs a day his whole life."

She nodded. "I never knew my father. He left my mom and I when I was just little."

"You said your mother died fifteen years ago?"

"She committed suicide when I was twelve. Slit her wrists in the bathtub, like something you'd see in a horror movie."

"Shit. That must have been tough."

"I made a lot of stupid choices as a teenager. I acted out—petty stuff. Vandalism, truancy, smoking pot." She looked down at her tea. "A whole lot of self-destructive behaviors, really. Then, one day, I met someone—a complete stranger. And, well, she helped me find ways to channel my emotions in a more positive way."

Did she find you passed out on a bench? "Is that what you're trying to do for me?"

Sierra seemed to pride herself on speaking with intention, careful to select words that would achieve the greatest impact. She took a long slurp of her tea, most likely giving thought to how she would formulate her response. It seemed disingenuous on some level, but a welcome change to the impulsive way most people communicated. "I see some of my former self in you, like I said. And I'd like to help."

Drew couldn't be certain if he was ready for help—not from her or anyone else. His life felt as though it was spiraling out of control, but he waffled between fearing it and celebrating it. "I'm not so big on emotions." He looked away. "So I'm not sure you could help me channel much of anything at the moment."

"Are you saying you're some kind of psychopath?"

"No, nothing like that—"

"Because a lot of salespeople have psychopathic tendencies."

Hot as it was, Drew swallowed the rest of his coffee in two big gulps. "I just mean that I don't feel things the way other people do."

"Maybe you've never allowed yourself to."

"I used to see therapists when I was young—"

"Sadness Doctors?" she asked, referencing their conversation at the park.

"Yeah, right. Sadness Doctors."

"Did it help?"

"I don't remember. Just one, who I nicknamed Coffee Breath—for obvious reasons. She encouraged me to keep a diary."

"Did that help?"

A shit-ton, yeah. Drew didn't feel comfortable mentioning his video diary entries just yet. They were private—Coffee Breath had insisted on it. "I don't think it helped much."

"We all handle tragedy differently, dude. Some of us lash out and some of us bottle it."

"I think I'm the latter."

"If that's the case, I understand why emotions are hard for you. You've numbed yourself to make room for the grief you carry."

"Maybe." All this self-analysis made Drew tense. It was foreign, enemy territory. A devastating descent into his own personal purgatory. "Did you ever find out why your mom ended her life?"

"I think coping with loneliness got the better of her, to be frank. She always blamed herself for my father leaving. She liked to bottle things, too."

"You never got to say goodbye either, I guess." Drew thought for a moment. "Is that part of the reason why you're so anxious to help others—to prevent suicides?"

Sierra seemed surprised at the leap he had made. "Yes, that's part of it, I imagine. But not just suicide. People do all sorts of harmful things when they can't accept reality."

"What sorts of things?"

"Substance abuse, for example. Drinking and drugs."

Don't forget gambling. "You said at the park that you don't drink." Drew had never met someone who purposefully refused alcohol.

"That's right, I don't. Not anymore, at least. I used to. I'd pop pills and drink by myself almost every night, wishing the world would come to an end."

Sounds like my kind of party.

"But it got me nowhere," she continued. "I gave up all that junk and took up running. If I ever got the urge to drink, I'd go for a jog. I keep fit and work out daily. I eat well—vegetarian, mostly organic and whole foods. And I work hard at my job. That's what I mean by channeling my emotions toward something positive."

"Do you like your job?"

"I do, actually. People usually think of accountants as boring types—"

Let me guess. You're the fun accountant.

"—but I find my career challenging and rewarding. I make good money and live comfortably."

"You must if you live in this neighborhood."

"I try to surround myself with likeminded people. It keeps me grounded."

Drew shuddered at the thought of a place where everyone was like Logan.

"Or," Sierra continued, "you can get your fill of drugs, alcohol, and meaningless sex—from Kara or whoever else. I get it. Change is hard. It takes time."

"Did you ever find yourself addicted?"

She studied his face, searching for the motivation behind his question.

"I'm just not sure I could give up drinking right now," Drew said.

"Addictions are choices, dude—nothing more. It's a hard battle, don't get me wrong, but it's up to you what you put in your body."

She makes it sound so easy.

"Trust me," she said. "I've battled my own . . . demons. If I can do it, you can, too."

Drew felt his phone vibrate again and pulled it from his pocket. He expected to see a text from Kara, but it was an incoming call from Transtel.

"Sorry," Drew said, raising his index finger. "It's work. I gotta get this."

She smiled politely.

"Hello?"

"Can I speak to Drew please?"

"Yes, this is Drew." He forced his voice to sound hoarse.

"Drew, it's Paul. Is everything okay?"

"I'm, uh, not feeling so good, Paul." Drew glanced at a clock across the room. He and Sierra had been talking for nearly an hour.

"What's all that noise in the background?" Hungry Paul asked.

"Oh, I—I'm just at the doctor's office in the waiting room."

Sierra rolled her eyes.

"Right," Hungry Paul replied. "Listen, we all need a personal day every now and again, but if you don't call in to the sick line an hour before your shift starts, it's considered a no-call, no-show."

"I'm sorry, Paul. My mistake."

"It's your first week taking calls, so I'll let it slide this time. Just remember for the future, okay?"

The future. The whole damn world is obsessed with the future. "You bet," Drew said. "Thanks for understanding. I hope to be back to normal tomorrow." The call ended and Drew tossed his phone on the table.

"That's your day off, huh? Calling in sick?"

"A day off is a day off," he replied.

Sierra raised her mug to her mouth, finishing her tea, the sleeve of her blouse retracting from her forearm. Drew caught a glimpse of her wrists for the first time—each one decorated with a detailed row of fine scars. She caught his line of sight. "I told you, dude. We've all got demons to face."

He nodded, his face grim and sympathetic.

"Sorry, but I have to get going. I'd be happy to continue chatting, though, if you're up for it later." She picked up his phone and entered her number in his contacts. "If you need help, please call me. You don't have to be alone."

Drew took back his phone and put it in his pocket. "I'll do that."

"I mean it, don't be a stranger. Let's get together again sometime soon—as long as Kara won't mind, that is."

"I told you. She's not my girlfriend."

"But she is willing to sleep with you, isn't she?"

Drew nodded in agreement.

"In my experience, for most men, that's the same thing." Sierra got to her feet, picking up both of their empty mugs from the table. Just before turning around, she said, "One last thing."

"What's that?"

"It isn't too late for you."

Drew had no idea what that meant.

"You agreed to have coffee with me," she explained. "I think you want to change—you just don't know how yet."

"Is that something I can figure out how to do—how to change, I mean?"

She raised her hands at her sides, a mug grasped in each, a gesticulation of uncertainty. "No idea. You'll change when the time is right—when you're ready. Takes a special moment, usually." She returned their mugs to the front counter and left Cool Beans.

Chapter 19

After having coffee with Sierra that morning, Drew ventured into a nearby thrift shop. He selected a few affordable items that his apartment lacked—a used set of bed sheets, a small desk for his laptop, and a decorative lamp. As though upgrading his humble abode might be the catalyst needed to make more difficult changes.

It hadn't occurred to Drew before checking out that he had left his car at the hospital the night before. He walked back to get it—deciding against visiting his father, still processing what he had learned the night before—then returned to the store to pick up his purchases. He wasn't sure the desk would fit—it took him twenty minutes to get it loaded in his hatchback. It turned out that even making small improvements could be difficult.

Once home, he did a load of laundry—his building housed coin operated laundry machines for communal use. He placed his new sheets on the mattress and relocated it to his bedroom. He moved his mountain bike to the balcony and placed the desk against the living room wall, setting the lamp on one of its dusty corners. He folded his pile of clothes in the bedroom closet, and stacked all his scattered boxes together in one place.

The Tuesday afternoon sun was pounding through his living room windows, which were still deprived of curtains.

He stood back and surveyed the changes he had made to his apartment, arriving at a simple conclusion—nothing was any different. There he was, still alone and craving a drink. He'd been sober only a few hours, yet the compulsion to imbibe gnawed at his insides, filling him with a familiar dull ache. It was beginning to feel like his entire interaction with Sierra that morning had been part of a broken dream sequence.

She had unloaded a lot of free advice, and some of it may have been valid. But it seemed trite and intangible at that moment. He only knew how to be himself, after all—flawed, distant, and cold. If he knew how to be anyone else, he'd have already auditioned for the role. Her words had reinforced a simple truth—that talk is cheap.

Drew received a notification on his phone—a new text message from Neil.

Neil: *Party at my new place Saturday night bro. Be there*

Neil: *Bring your call center bitch if you want*

Drew hadn't considered bringing Kara to Neil's housewarming party. He liked the idea of showing her off, but Neil could be a bit much, as could the parties he threw.

He set himself on his rocking chair, carefully examining the desk for the first time. It was outdated, worn and chipped, but better than nothing. Drew stared at his laptop, eager to record a new entry in his video diary. A lot had happened in the last twenty-four hours, so much so that hitting the record button seemed daunting. He couldn't decide where to begin, so he allowed his mind to wander.

Sierra had offered him a word of caution about his pseudo relationship with Kara—not all that glitters is gold.

Easy for her to say. She's done a lot of fucking and I haven't.

Kara had added a certain bounce to his step in recent history. She had given him a reason to feel normal on some level. He even felt lusted after, which was an abnormal sensation. Sure, Heather had made him feel wanted, but in a clingy, codependent way. Kara seemed to desire him on a primal, visceral level. A new and entirely welcomed experience.

It seemed that living with purpose, as Sierra might have described it, meant forsaking the few things that brought him joy. And a joyless life seemed like all the more reason to get drunk and high—a sort of vicious circle that he wasn't sure how to break, even if he wanted to.

A knock came at the door—an unusual knock with an unfamiliar pattern.

Drew opened up. "What's with the fancy knock?"

"That's my new top secret knock," Marcus said. "It's kinda like a secret handshake. I came up with it so my customers will know it's me."

"But I just called. I was pretty sure it was you."

"Ah, that's a good point. So can I come in?" Drew held the door open and Marcus moseyed into his newly ornamented living space. "Where'd your bed go?"

"It's in the bedroom now, believe it or not."

"Right, that makes sense." Marcus snapped his fingers, noticing the new piece of furniture against the wall. "You got a desk, too."

Drew had found Marcus bothersome when they had first met. His lackadaisical approach to distributing illicit substances was baffling. But Drew was starting to find his quirkiness refreshing, almost endearing. If only all merchants were so personable and free of judgment. The crowd at Cool Beans could learn something from him.

Marcus handed him a baggie. Drew held it in his palm for the longest time, staring at its powdered contents, and it seemed to make Marcus uncomfortable. "Are you going to pay me?" he finally asked. "This is usually the part where you give me some money and tell me to leave."

Drew nodded, but felt torn. He reached in his pocket and grabbed all the cash he had left, counting out enough to keep himself fed until Friday, his first payday at Transtel, and handed over the rest. "Is that enough?"

"A little short, but you can give me the rest later."

It only took me a week to get myself into debt with my new dealer.

He saluted Drew and headed for the door. "See you soon. Call me anytime."

Drew scrutinized the coke in his hand. If this were a movie, this is the part where he'd go flush it, determined to make his life right again. But this wasn't a movie, it was something much worse—real life. And the sad truth was that no matter what he did with the coke, snort it or flush it, it wasn't going to make a bit of difference. Not today, anyway.

His phone vibrated again.

Kara: *Are you feeling better?*

Drew debated how to respond. His head wasn't whirling anymore and his stomach had slowed its churning, but he still felt rattled and out of sorts.

Drew: *Yes. I'm doing better now thank you*

Kara: *Good. I have something for you*

An incoming image download. It was a selfie of Kara in the Transtel restroom—where she'd performed oral sex on him the day before—standing in front of the mirror, lifting her shirt.

Kara: *I'm horny ;)*

Kara: *Come fuck me right here in the bathroom*

Kara: *This place is so boring when you're not here*

Drew: *You're making me hard*

Kara: *Show me*

Drew complied, dropping his pants and snapping a quick

photo with his phone. Even if he had spent all his twenties single, he couldn't imagine a scenario in which he would have volunteered snapshots of his genitals to women. As he understood it, most of them didn't care for that sort of thing. But in this case, Kara had asked for it.

More to the point, his penis wasn't anything special. It was a bit on the small side, and definitely crooked—too much masturbation the most likely culprit. Not to mention he put no effort into keeping his pubic hair trimmed. He knew sending an image of his depressing appendage wasn't likely to generate much interest from the opposite sex, but considering the day before, there was no harm in letting Kara have another peek.

Kara: *Yum! :) Can't wait to feel it inside me*

Kara: *I'm gonna milk you dry*

Drew: *How do you want me to give it to you?*

Kara: *From behind is my fave, plus the view should be good for you*

Kara: *But you can give it to me any way you want*

Kara: *Just make sure to pull my hair and smack me around a bit*

Drew wasn't sure what to make of this. His only sexual experiences in the past five years had been with Heather—boring, unresponsive, and missionary. Slow, near silent, and always with the lights out and a condom on. Never more than once a week. A predictable routine that ran like clockwork.

Drew wondered if Kara would ever be like Sierra, one day recounting the copious amounts of casual sex she once had. Taking it however she could get it, even from her coworker with the tiny bent penis.

I'm probably being too hard on myself.

Then again, if Kara were anything like Sierra had been, looking to fill some kind of inner void, she would probably enjoy some blow. He snapped a photo of the baggie and sent it to her.

Drew: *You into nose candy?*

Kara: *I'm into whatever you are Drew Thomson ;)*

Kara: *Lol*

Kara: *It's been a while but yes I'd love a hit of that*

Drew: *It's gonna be a fun night*

Kara: *You have no idea. ;) xoxo*

Drew dropped the baggie in his desk drawer and grabbed his two towels, wedging them below the apartment and balcony doors. It was becoming a familiar procedure.

He would save the coke for tomorrow night—but in the meantime, some weed might settle his mind. He rolled a small joint and sparked it up, finally ready to record.

"I found out last night that Dad isn't who I thought he was . . . "

He sucked in a lungful of smoke, held it deep, and exhaled it slowly.

"He's—he's not a bad guy, I don't think. I'm just seeing him in a, uh, different way now. I mean, I don't think he's a bigot or whatever. He's just a product of his time. The world changed around him and he didn't change with it."

Even Drew had a tough time believing that. Being old fashioned was one thing, but a father shutting out his son was another. He wasn't ready to believe that his father could be so severe. Distant, sure, but certainly not the confrontational type. And not the sort of man to take a position on much of anything.

"I think I owe it to Logan to give him another shot. He's an asshole for sure, but maybe there's more to the story. Dad always accepted me though, just as I was. I never had to be something else. But I guess Logan never felt that kind of acceptance. And I can't imagine what life would be like without someone there to make me feel normal."

It occurred to Drew that perhaps his father, from an era long gone, was a human warning sign. A reminder of the tragedy that seemed to follow a life unfulfilled.

"Dad spent the last twenty years waiting for his life to end, and maybe I've been doing the same thing. I met this chick at Northwood Park this morning, and she was just bursting at the seams to tell me all about her own life. Her mother killed herself a long time ago and yet—I don't know, she, uh, reacted differently than I did when Mom died. She used it as a reason to help others."

Maybe she's just as fucked as I am, and maybe she's just pretending to be all right.

"I don't know if I could ever do that. Help others like she does. I'm too selfish, I think. It's pitiful, I know, but I couldn't be bothered." He ran his fingers through his scraggly facial hair. "But then again, where did that get Dad?"

Drew took another pull, the smoke taking the edge off, aiding his concentration. He struggled to articulate what was really on his mind. He needed a drink, and as soon as possible. It was four o'clock in the afternoon. Had he been at work, he would have already finished his water bottle.

"The truth is, after talking to her, I thought maybe I was ready to change. Even, uh, came home and straightened the place up a bit." *Go ahead, you fucking junkie. Explain why it's all too hard.* "But, uh, not yet . . . I'm not ready, I don't think. Maybe some other time. I mean, I've got my whole god-damn life to change."

The nagging sense of failure at turning his life around that morning wore at him, but only for the briefest of moments. Nothing a drink wouldn't fix.

"She said something else to me this morning, something that I haven't heard in a long time. Sierra talked about special moments, and that was a phrase Coffee Breath used to use with me." *But what do they know? They aren't you.*

He thought hard about what Coffee Breath had told him as a child.

"She told me every moment was special in its own way, and that keeping this diary would help me . . . live my truth, whatever that means. I'm just not sure what to believe anymore. It's like everyone has their own little recipe for happiness, but no one really seems all that happy."

Drew found that realization both disturbing and profound. He second-guessed himself, hoping his observation had been inaccurate.

"I've got Kara coming over tomorrow night, even though Sierra thinks casual sex leaves us feeling hollow. Something like that, even though she used to get around plenty. Who knows? Maybe fucking leads to some sort of enlightenment. It's worth finding out . . . "

He inhaled all he could from what remained of the joint, setting it in a glass ashtray as the flame reached the paper filter at its end.

"I just hope I don't embarrass myself when she comes over. Kara is so hot, and I think she's got a little more practice than I do."

Drew felt a bit strange, a grown man of twenty-eight, intimidated at the thought of getting together with an attractive woman. He hoped his insecurities wouldn't show tomorrow night.

Having said all he intended to, Drew ended the recording at four minutes and ten seconds. On the inside—buried right around where Sierra had tapped him on the chest earlier that day—he knew he had more to share. Reality was starting to bubble to the surface: he wasn't living his truth at all, no matter how many special moments he shared with his webcam. But he wasn't ready to admit it to himself.

Drew dug through his neatly arranged boxes, scattering them across the living room, frantic, searching for a bottle of whiskey. He knew it was in there somewhere. *Got you, you little bastard.* He opened it and tipped it back, relieving the irritation coursing through his blood.

He opened a new browser tab and navigated to his favorite online poker site. He deposited the few dollars that remained in his checking account and joined a virtual table, where he spent the rest of the day.

Chapter 20

Kara had been telling the truth—she did indeed sleep naked. But after she and Drew had consumed nearly a half gram of cocaine, neither one achieved rejuvenating slumber.

They got up the next morning, jittery and unrested, and began the awkward dance of readying themselves for work in the presence of a stranger. Both were in dire need of a shower, drenched in a curious cocktail of bodily fluids, their nether regions sore from friction.

After a quick stop for breakfast at a rundown Palmer Heights diner, they drove their respective cars to Transtel, arriving at work minutes before their scheduled starts.

Drew stole the occasional glance at Kara, his mind working to make sense of what had happened the night before. Their sex date had felt like a performance, as though Kara had been reciting the lines to her favorite pornographic films, her voice a high-pitched squeal at all times. Enjoyable, for sure, but false at the same time—almost too good to be true. Drew couldn't shake the feeling that he and Kara had been unified by lonesomeness rather than intimacy.

Kara peeked over at Drew every so often, offering him a debauched smile or a suggestive wink. An hour or so into their shift, she tossed him a folded note. *My ass hurts*, it read in her handwriting, her signature heart beneath it.

At nearly eleven o'clock, Hungry Paul approached Drew,

a serious look on his face.

"Good morning, Paul. How's it going?"

"Good, thanks. You're not on a call, are you?"

Obviously not, dickhead. I'm talking to you. "No, sir. Not at the moment."

"Good. Can you drop yourself out of queue and join me in my office?"

Drew did as he was asked, following Hungry Paul to a secluded cubicle against the far wall of the call center floor. Hardly an office, but it was where Hungry Paul spent most of his time, hiding out behind artificial walls and scanning reports.

I bet he masturbates to photos of cheeseburgers back here, too.

Hungry Paul spoke first. "Are you feeling better?"

"Yeah, stomach bug on Tuesday. I spent the morning puking." Hungry Paul remained silent, giving Drew a chance to elaborate. "I'm, uh, sorry about not calling in before my shift. I was feeling pretty rough."

"I understand. How's your dad doing?"

Since visiting his father with Logan Monday night, Drew hadn't returned to the hospital. Two full days without checking in, but he had every intention to visit that night—and to hopefully confront his father about what had transpired between he and Logan all those years before.

"He's not doing so great. Won't be with us much longer."

"I'm sorry to hear that," Hungry Paul said, unmoved. "Listen, I want to talk to you about your relationship with Kara Davenport."

"My relationship?"

"You told me when I interviewed you that you have your sights set on management."

I lied. "I do."

"All right, well, let me put it to you this way—do you

152

think a candidate for management should be fooling around with other agents?"

"Of course not, but there's nothing going on between me and Kara. And even if there was, I'm not a candidate for management already, am I?"

"It's called professionalism, Drew. You're always being evaluated."

I can't believe this fat fuck is going to school me on professionalism. He's a manager at a call center for crying out loud.

"You need to show up for the job you want, not the job you have," Hungry Paul explained.

"I agree with you, sir, but this is the first I'm hearing of concerns with my performance."

He shook his head and rotated his computer monitor toward Drew. "Do you see that?"

"I'm not sure what I'm looking at, to be honest."

"These are some of the reports I review daily—handle times, time in and out of queue, and the like. It gives me a sense of who my top performers are."

"Am I one of them?"

"Today will be your third shift." He pointed at a chart on the screen. "You haven't had to escalate a single call to me. Meanwhile most of your peers are escalating four or five angry callers a day."

"I'm good at taking shit, I guess."

"You're always back from lunch early. You often skip breaks—"

"All I do is sit in one place," Drew said with a shrug. "No need for a break."

"Yet it looks like you spent twelve minutes out of queue on Monday."

Shit!

"Monday, three twelve to three twenty-four—"

"I had to use the bathroom."

"Uh huh. It looks like Ms. Davenport had to use the bathroom at the exact same time."

"She did?"

"Yeah, and do you know the strangest part?"

"We both ate the cafeteria food?"

"Around that same time Monday, one of your coworkers returned from the women's bathroom and reported that two of her coworkers were fornicating inside a stall."

Bubbles, that cunt. Drew shook his head, feigning surprise. "Did you ever find out who it was in there?"

"I have a pretty good idea," Hungry Paul said with a grin. "I watched you and Ms. Davenport pass notes to each other all through training. I've noticed you take your lunch breaks together. And this morning I saw you come skipping in together, hand in hand, for the whole building to see."

"We weren't holding hands."

"You're treading a fine line, Drew. You received a copy of the employee handbook, right?"

"I believe so."

"There's no provision against being friends with your colleagues, even outside of work. But sexual activity is prohibited onsite, of course, and managers are discouraged from engaging in romantic relationships with subordinates. Not to mention . . . " He peeked over the cubicle wall, ensuring they had privacy, " . . . I've noticed that you and Ms. Davenport sometimes share a water bottle."

"Yeah, she's so forgetful like that. Always leaving hers at home."

"I know you came from the corporate world, Drew, and next to other managers you've worked for, you probably think I'm an idiot."

You got me.

He didn't wait for Drew to respond. "But I'm not stupid. Employees don't share a water bottle at work unless there's something good in it."

"It sounds to me like you know your mineral waters, Paul."

"It sounds to me like getting drunk on the job is grounds for immediate termination."

"Good thing I'm stone sober."

"Yes, that is a good thing."

It wasn't that Drew thrived on resisting authority, nor did he resent it—he generally preferred to slip under the radar, to be agreeable and avoid confrontation when possible. But at this exact moment, called out for his drinking, he found the temptation to push back irresistible.

"Paul, I have to ask—where's this conversation going? If you suspect I'm banging your agents, drinking on the job, and playing hooky, why not just fire me?"

"Is that what you want?"

Drew thought for a moment. *I need this job, at least for the time being . . . unless Marcus is hiring.* "No."

"It's not what I want either. You have a lot of potential, and if you work hard, I think you could make an excellent manager here someday. And so far you've made my job easy. In defense of Ms. Davenport, so has she—you're two of my better agents. I wouldn't want to lose either of you, but I can only turn a blind eye for so long."

Drew sunk his head in defeat. He was no fan of Hungry Paul, but he received his message loud and clear.

"What I'd like you to do," Hungry Paul concluded, "is to listen carefully to what I'm telling you, clean up your act, and live up to your potential."

He sounds like Sierra. "I can do that, Paul. Thanks for the talk."

"You're welcome."

Drew returned to his workstation, taking a moment to digest their conversation before putting his headset back on. He glanced at Kara. Her hair wasn't fashioned with its usual care, her clothes were wrinkled, and her makeup had been applied with haste. Even her customary scent was missing. She was still gorgeous, of course, but she wore plain evidence of their shenanigans the night before. Drew wondered to himself why he had ever thought their involvement could be kept secret, obvious about it as they were.

She caught him staring. "What was that all about?"

"Nothing. Just some paperwork I forgot to fill out in training."

"What paperwork?"

"Nothing important. Listen, what are you up to Saturday night?"

"This weekend?"

Drew nodded.

Kara rocked her head back and forth for a second or two. "I'm free, I think. Why? Think you can handle me for another night?"

"As a matter of fact, I'd love another night with you, and my friend Neil happens to be having a housewarming party. He just moved in, and I haven't seen his new place yet. Want to come with me?"

"A real date, Drew Thomson?" She looked stunned. "You actually want to be seen in public with me?"

What do I have to lose?

Chapter 21

Russell stirred, restless and agitated, slowly opening his eyes. Drew perched at his bedside. The television mounted on the opposite wall relayed a muted news broadcast of weather reports with stock tickers peeling across the bottom.

"You're awake," Drew said. He had arrived at the hospital shortly after work, determined to talk to his father. Hours had passed and his patience had paid off.

Following his chat with Hungry Paul, Drew had felt obliged to put away his water bottle for the remainder of the workday. But the ride over to the hospital had given him a chance to restore balance, having consumed enough vodka to pacify his frayed nerves for a few hours.

"Drew . . . " Russell trailed off, his speech slurred, strained and arduous.

Patrick had been in and out of the room all night, and he was currently visiting with his family downstairs, granting Drew time alone with his father.

Drew stood and made eye contact with Russell who looked tortured, miserable, his life force depleted. "How are you feeling?"

"I feel like I'm ready to die." Russell glared at the mashed dinner that had been set on his bedside table. He turned away from it, making his disgust obvious.

"I'm sorry you have to go through this."

"Nothing to be sorry for. It's time."

"Is that really how you feel?"

Russell fought to breathe, shifting himself on the bed, as though inhaling from different positions might lessen his discomfort. "I told you, son. I'm ready to go."

"Has Logan been coming to see you?"

"He's come a few times now."

"I talked to him the other day."

"S'pose another fist fight broke out between you two."

"Dad, I found out Logan is gay."

Russell closed his eyes in annoyance, Drew observing his reaction. "Logan isn't gay," he said at last. "Never was."

"Dad, Logan is married to—"

"I know who he's married to." He spluttered and hacked, small droplets of blood collecting at the corners of his mouth. "That fairy friend of his, Stephen. We've met. See, that's the world we live in now, son. We let a man sodomize another man and call it marriage."

I sodomized a woman last night, and nobody seems to mind that.

"Is it true, Dad? That you threw Logan out when he was a teenager?"

Russell's eyes twitched, his mind calculating a response. "I didn't throw him out. I just told him he had to act right if he wanted to live under my roof."

"Act right?"

More coughing, wetter this time. "Logan's no faggot queen. He knows better. Says his mother always knew he was queer, but Angie woulda never stood for that."

She wouldn't have?

"You got real quiet after your mom passed, son. You stuck close to home, kept to yourself, minded your own damn business. Logan went the other direction—putting on a show for everybody, loud and proud and all that. Shopping in the women's department, heading off to his fancy school with a bunch of fags, kikes, and liberals."

"And you hate him for that?"

"I don't hate him. I'm sickened by it, that's all. Look, he wasn't always this way, and people don't change. People like—"

Like you and me?

"—like you and me," Russell explained, gasping for air. "I told you, there's two kinds of guys in this world . . . "

"Guys who act like they're in control, and guys who accept life as it is. Something like that."

"You've been taking notes."

"So what're you saying?" Drew asked. "Logan thinks he's in control when he's not?"

His father nodded. "Thinks he's special, different from the rest of us. That's what this is all about, you know. Thinking he can turn his back on who he is."

"You don't think people can change?" It was Drew's intention to discuss Logan, but at that moment, the topic at hand applied just as much to himself.

"Don't be a fool, son. Nobody changes. We're put on this earth to live our lives. We do it, some of us even learn to accept it. Then we die. That's it."

"What if I had been gay?"

"You're not."

"But what if I—"

"Damn it, Drew. You're not gay and neither is Logan. He's just looking for love and acceptance wherever he can get it. Seeking attention, that's all, like some kind of man whore."

"Did you ever think maybe he's looking for love and acceptance, and you and I spent the last twenty years hiding from it?"

"Don't be ridiculous."

"Maybe Logan is . . . " Drew hesitated, " . . . living his truth. And maybe we've been denying ours."

"Now you're starting to sound like a fudge packer, too." Specks of red saliva trickled from his father's mouth. Drew handed him a wad of Kleenex to wipe his chin. "It's all going to be over soon, son, but remember what I'm about to tell you. We're all here to do one thing in this life." He was trailing off, fatigued from their brief exchange. "And that one thing . . . "

"Dad?"

"Accept . . . "

"Accept what?"

"Accept it. All of it. Don't change it. Remember that . . . "

Drew felt his face burning, his eyes swelling with moisture. "I love you, Dad."

Russell returned to medicated rest.

Drew stood at his father's bedside for what felt like hours before making his way to the stairwell of the hospital, phone clutched in hand. He rocked in place, soothing his inner volatility and staring at the wall. He sent a short text message and waited for a reply.

Chapter 22

Sierra was on the same bench when Drew arrived, her height unmistakable even when seated. She saw him approaching and got to her feet, outfitted in loose-fitting attire and running shoes, extending her long arms for a giant hug. "Hi, Drew. It's good to see you again."

Drew wasn't big on friendly embraces, least of all in public, dismissing them as superficial and contrived. But he had been the one to invite Sierra out for a walk. It seemed only fair to be amenable to her greeting. He wrapped his arms around her, their bodies linking for an instant. "Good to see you, too. Thanks for coming."

"How are things going?"

He speculated that Sierra already knew the answer to her own question. If things were going swimmingly, he wouldn't have texted. "Things are going all right, I guess."

They set off on foot, their pace brisker than their Tuesday excursion, and followed the paved trail, their shadows elongated under dim lamplight.

"How's Kara?"

"Uh, good. Thanks for asking."

"Did you sleep with her yet?"

"Jesus, you just get right to it, don't you?"

"I'm no good at small talk, dude. And neither are you."

"Good point." A late night jogger passed them, but the

trail was otherwise vacant in both directions. "She came over last night."

"Nice. Did she let you put it in her butt?"

If Drew were prone to blushing, he might have done so at that moment. "Uh, yes, actually, how did—"

She interrupted Drew with a high five. "Was it your first time entering a woman through the back door?"

"Yeah."

"Did you like it?"

"I mean, sure, what's not to like? It's warm and tight and a lot like forbidden fruit."

"And she didn't make you wrap it up, did she?"

"Jesus, Sierra. Were you peeking through the windows or something?"

Sierra laughed. "No, just a series of lucky guesses, that's all. And I'm not judging you. I'm happy for you. If hooking up with Kara makes you happy, go for it."

"It was a bit like banging a porn star. I mean, Jesus, how many issues of *Cosmo* does a woman have to read to learn how to fuck like that?"

"Practice makes perfect."

"I guess so." Drew shifted his gaze toward the effervescent night sky. "You know, I'm a little surprised at your reaction. The whole time we were going at it, all I could think of was how much you'd probably disapprove."

She stopped walking. "You were thinking of me while you were inside your girlfriend?"

"She's not my girlfriend."

Sierra smirked and resumed walking.

"How about you?" Drew asked. "Get any quality action lately?"

"Dude, I work all the damn time and when I'm not working, I'm usually reading or keeping active—"

162

"Or meeting strangers for a stroll at the park."

"Point is I don't have time for head games and one-night stands."

"Me and Kara aren't a one-night thing. She's coming with me to a friend's housewarming party Saturday night."

"Well, you said you hoped to fall in love with her. This could be your chance." She put her hands in her pockets. "Will there be drugs at the party?"

"Probably."

"Is Kara into drugs?"

"Kara's into pretty much whatever."

"I figured."

"You figured what?"

"Let me ask you something, Drew. Do you intend to spend the rest of your life with Kara?"

"What? No. We met just a couple weeks ago—how could I possibly know that?"

"Do you believe in love at first sight?"

"Of course not. It sounds like a cheesy Hallmark slogan."

"It does, but don't be so naïve. Ever spent a long time in the wrong relationship?"

"Yeah, my ex and I were together five years," Drew confessed.

"But you were drawn to Kara instantly, right?"

"Are you saying I should save sex for marriage or something? Didn't take you for a religious nut."

"Oh, God no, not at all. Have sex with anyone you wish, and definitely don't marry someone for the wrong reasons. I'm just wondering what's special about Kara. Why take her to a party when you could probably just hook up with someone there?"

"I . . . like Kara. And she's insanely hot."

"But you don't love her."

"The closest I've ever come to loving someone is my dad, and, well, I don't think that's the same thing."

"Sure. But my point is that you and her aren't exclusive. There'd be no harm in meeting someone new at the party, but you want to bring her anyway." Sierra dragged her feet for a moment. "Can I be honest with you?"

"I'm starting to learn it's the only thing you know how to be."

"I think Kara's like a drug. She's intoxicating. She overwhelms your senses and clouds your judgment, kinda like a dose of heroin. She keeps you content for a while, almost like getting high, but she leaves your system sooner or later, and then you come crashing back down to reality."

That's one theory.

"So why did you ask to see me tonight?" Sierra asked.

"I just came from visiting Dad."

"And he isn't doing so good?"

"He's not, but that's not it. I found out my brother is gay and Dad kicked him out when he was teenager."

"That's awful."

"I asked him about it tonight. I wanted to know if it was true and why he would do that."

"He probably wasn't comfortable with the idea of change."

Drew considered her suggestion. "That's basically what he said—that Logan was only acting out for attention. And right before falling asleep, he left me with one final piece of advice. To accept life as it is and never to try and change it."

"Powerful stuff."

"You think so?"

"I was being facetious," she said with a quiet laugh.

"Oh."

"It takes no power at all to be exactly the same person."

She let out a dramatic sigh. "Sorry, I'm not trying to bad-mouth your dad."

"I know. It's just that I've spent my whole life learning from his example. And I'm only realizing now that maybe it wasn't such a good idea. I thought he was content, just a simple man, happy to be left to his own devices. But I'm figuring out that he was actually pretty miserable for the most part."

Sierra absorbed his thoughts in what seemed like intro-spective solace, staring at the ground, apparently enthralled by the patter of their footsteps. "Let me ask you something. Earlier you told me you don't want to spend your whole life with Kara. You just met her, you don't know her all that well. That's what you said, right?"

"Something like that."

"Because you have your whole life ahead of you."

"And thinking about the future upsets me."

She nodded. "But put yourself in your dad's shoes, back when he lost your mom. Do you think he decided right then and there to be miserable for the rest of his life?"

"Probably not."

"Right. People rarely make a choice knowing it might ruin their entire lives."

"Where are you going with this?"

"Dude, what I'm trying to tell you is that happiness isn't something you work toward, the same way misery isn't something you work toward. Neither arrives in the mail ten or twenty years down the road. They're both achieved in the moment, special moments, small moments, one at a time, all strung together. They're the end result of the choices we make."

It took Drew a moment to process her philosophical con-siderations.

"Your dad didn't plan to be miserable until the day he died. He just allowed himself to be miserable every day and it became a pattern. A habit of sorts. And those habits become our lives."

"You're saying Dad should have just magically started being happy every day instead of being miserable?"

"I'm saying that change is hard, but each day is a new opportunity for change. It's filled with moments, chances to make tough choices and pursue whatever brings us joy."

"You're right about one thing for sure—change is hard."

"Change is hard until you have a reason to change." She delayed her next thought, giving it emphasis. "Ask yourself—is Kara your reason to change?"

Drew shook his head.

"How about the drugs, the booze—do they give you motivation to change?"

"No."

"Does your dad encourage you to change?"

"Definitely not."

"Once you know why you want to change, the rest gets a lot easier."

Drew and Sierra had completed the loop of the short trail twice now, passing the bench again, continuing on for a third lap.

"Let me ask *you* something," he blurted out at once, apprehensive.

"All right."

"Why did you approach me on this bench?"

"You looked like you needed help."

"I don't think you're being completely honest with me."

"I like to feed the ducks."

"Sierra, please."

"If I dug deep enough, I'd say I felt drawn to you, like I

knew we probably had a lot in common."

"You got all that from seeing me passed out drunk on a park bench?"

"I figured we'd have a good chat at the very least."

"Good how?"

She turned to face Drew. "Look at me, dude. I'm a five foot eleven Barbie doll with blonde hair, blue eyes, and big tits." Drew's line of sight darted to her chest, which was guarded by a baggy sweatshirt. "I keep them hidden, my friend, because the last thing I need is extra attention. I stick out everywhere I go. I intimidate women and men objectify me. And let's not forget that I've built a reputation for myself around certain parts of town. So if I were to answer your question with complete honesty? I seek out people who I can have a real conversation with. People who enjoy talking about real things that actually matter."

"What do you mean by things that matter?" They resumed walking, faster than before.

"Life and death, dude. Growth, change, empowerment, becoming your best self. The sort of thing you accused me of borrowing from a Tony Robbins book."

"Can I share something with you?" Drew asked. He hesitated, then added, "I've never told this to anyone."

"Go right ahead."

"I've always believed, right or wrong, that life churns forward toward some kind of preordained outcome—a foregone conclusion, I guess. Something we can't control."

"Sounds depressing."

"Maybe. But what I've begun to realize is that the people we meet along the way can influence the outcome, for better or worse."

Sierra listened, offering Drew her undivided attention.

"The outcome doesn't always change, but sometimes our

perspectives do. Like the asshole that killed Mom. He changed my life and he didn't even know it. The Sadness Doctor I met as a child—"

"Coffee Breath?"

"Yeah, her. People have a way of entering our lives without warning and departing the same way. And each of them leaves behind a piece of him or herself—a lot like a mishmash of different colors of Play-Doh. I guess what I've always been unclear on is whether I'm supposed to reshape that blob of Play-Doh into something new, or if I'm supposed to just appreciate the blob for what it is."

"You want my opinion?"

"Yes, of course."

"Put the Play-Doh in a jar and find something else to do. Focus on the real world around you and spend your time on something constructive."

Their third loop was complete. They stopped in front of the bench. "Thanks for spending some time with me tonight," Drew said.

"My pleasure. I told you. I'm a big fan of deep talk, pouring out feelings, whatever you've got time for."

"One last thing."

"Shoot."

"What's my reason to change?"

"You have to figure that one out yourself. And you will, when you're ready."

"That's what you told me last time we met."

"It's still early—if you're not ready to change tonight, maybe you could give Kara a booty call."

Drew knew Sierra was joking, but he scowled under his breath.

"Oh, lighten up, dude."

"I think I like Kara because she likes me."

"Did sleeping with her make you happy?"

"At the time."

"Keep your chin up," she said with a nod. "You're only human."

Sierra was attractive, sure, but her best features were more than skin deep—her spirit, her wit, her boldness, her intuition, her undeniably strong conversation skills. He found himself at a loss to explain why she seemed to enjoy his company. Was he a pet project for her, an incomplete being in need of repair? Or was it possible that she, a strong, capable, and assertive woman, actually liked spending time with him?

"Would you . . . " He trailed off.

"Huh?"

"Would you ever date someone like me?"

"What do you mean someone like you?"

"I'm flawed and broken. I'm fucked up. You're not, at least not anymore."

"I wouldn't date an alcoholic or a drug user if that's what you mean."

"What if I changed?"

"Don't make me your reason to change." Sierra looked stern, almost angry. "You have to find your own reason. And I'm not promising you anything. I like our talks, Drew, and I think we could be great friends. Don't mess that up."

Drew ignored her warning and leaned inward, motivated by an unexpected surge of bravery, planting a clumsy peck on her cheek.

She pulled away at first, stunned. "Drew, what are you doing?"

"I don't know."

"Think about Kara."

"She's not my girlfriend, and you said you were drawn to

me."

"I was."

"You still are. That's why you agreed to meet me again tonight."

"Sure, I guess, but I think you're reading into it."

"Am I?"

She dawdled for a few seconds, unnerved, and then gave Drew a soft, sweet kiss on the lips, holding nothing back. It was the type of kiss that made it impossible for him to keep his eyes opened. It sent chills down his spine and filled his stomach with butterflies.

Sierra unlocked her lips from his after a moment and opened her eyes. "Goodnight, Drew. Let's do this again soon."

Chapter 23

It was Saturday, the third of July, and Drew was due to arrive for Neil's big celebration, eager to show up with Kara on his arm.

They passed through tall revolving doors and found themselves in a foyer that rivaled five-star hotels in decadence. Its interior was constructed of marble, an elegant grand piano at one end, high back winged chairs grouped together, separated by sculptures and other abstract works of modern art.

A mini security detail greeted them, collecting their personal details before allowing them to go further. After a brief exchange, the two guards on duty waved Drew through to the elevator bank, him wearing jeans and a faded polo shirt, his usual look of gracelessness about him.

Kara followed behind him, decked out in a one sleeve party dress that hugged her curves, heels and a handbag to match, the poise of rock star. She looked no worse for wear, despite consenting to a backseat romp with Drew on the way over. They stepped on to an elevator.

"You haven't told me anything about your friend yet," Kara said.

Ding. The elevator opened to more marble. Fresh cut flowers welcomed them from a crystal vase upon a stone pillar adjacent to the elevator door. Hanging globe lights and plush ruby carpet blazed a trail toward Neil's corner unit.

"Neil is, uh, a year older than me. We used to work together. He fancies himself a big shot of sorts and dresses the part."

Kara looked around. "I can tell."

"He, uh, does well with the ladies."

"Ooh, is he hot?"

"Why would you ask me that?"

"Oh, come on. Boys do it all the time. You even mention another girl and it's the first thing they ask, 'Is she hot?' So I'm asking you the same thing."

"He's a good looking guy."

"But no competition for you, right?" She winked.

"I never considered myself much of a looker."

Kara smacked Drew in the chest with her handbag, startling him. "Do I look like the kinda girl who'd hook up with an ugly guy?"

Yes. "No."

"Don't put yourself down like that, Drew Thomson." She leaned against him, grabbing his crotch and giving it a squeeze. "You're a decent looking guy." Another squeeze, this one almost painful. "And I want more of this later—give me a signal when it's time to go, and we'll head back to your place for round two."

Loud music and the smell of fresh paint emerged from the edges of Neil's door. Neil opened up and flashed his trademark smile. He looked like a listing agent at his own open house.

"You made it," he said to Drew. His eyes quickly shifted to Kara.

"Hi, Neil," Drew said, motioning to his date. "This is Kara. Kara, this is Neil."

Neil was dressed to impress, as anticipated—a matching

THE FIFTEENTH OF JUNE

suit jacket and trousers in navy blue, walnut brown shoes, and a crisp white shirt, freshly pressed. He reached for Kara, kissing the back of her hand. "Kara, it's wonderful to meet you. I had no idea you were so lovely."

She reacted with an elegant curtsy, her face brilliant, reflective of his compliment. "It's nice to meet you too, Neil. I've heard so much about you."

"Please, come in," Neil said, making a sweeping gesture.

Kara entered first, slowing down to take in her surroundings, her eyes wide with astonishment. Neil restrained Drew for a moment, holding him within earshot at the door. "You didn't tell me she was so fucking hot, bro."

"I tried to, but—"

"You hit that yet?"

"Yeah, a couple times now."

Neil slapped Drew on the shoulder. "That's what I'm talking about."

After obligatory small talk, Neil took Drew and Kara on an expedition, first nodding toward a number of uniformed caterers, and then a hired DJ. The condo itself was a bit like walking into the cover of an interior design magazine— glossy, uninhabitable, and two-dimensional. Neil made sure to exhibit his expensive furnishings, some still wrapped in plastic, as well as decorative embellishments and miscellaneous artifacts, each one straddling a fine line between sophisticated and tasteless. The twelve-foot ceilings, rife with pot lights, triggered echoes of his voice, ensuring no remark went unnoticed.

"Isn't it a bit big?" Drew asked. "You know, considering you live by yourself." Drew found himself out of his element, missing the sheer simplicity of his own dilapidated dwelling. *He never did visit my place, come to think of it.*

Neil looked equal parts revolted and insulted.

"I think it's perfect," Kara announced with glee. "You should be really proud, Neil."

"Looks like your woman has better taste than you do, bro." He punched Drew on the shoulder—too soft to inflict injury but too hard to be friendly. "Come on, let me introduce you to some people."

Neil marched onward to continue the tour, Kara at his heels.

The realization came to Drew at once that if Sierra were present, she would have deduced that Neil was compensating for something. Kara, by comparison, seemed enchanted by Neil's every word, salivating at the luxury around each corner.

The trio entered what was presumably a second living room, certainly much larger than the last. A double glass door swung open at its end onto a balcony, overlooking the urban landscape below. The room was filled with a dozen or so picture perfect socialites, mixing and mingling as if to reenact a beer commercial.

"I think you might recognize a few of these characters," Neil said to Drew, motioning toward some of his former colleagues from The Ascension Group.

Drew exchanged subtle nods and smiles with a selection of familiar faces—he hadn't made a lot of friends at his former job—then spotted a few characters who looked out of place. Private security contractors, it appeared. "Why do you have rent-a-cops here?"

Neil took Drew by the elbow, guiding him a few paces from Kara. "I hired a promoter to make sure we do this thing right. He's coming by later with some girls and things might get interesting. Plus I scored a few party favors for the ladies, if you know what I mean."

"I don't."

"Ketamine, ecstasy—bro, I don't know, whatever gets chicks in the mood to party." He eyed Kara. "There'll be plenty of quality tail to choose from tonight. If you were smart, you'd give her the night off."

Their sidebar ended without ceremony and they rejoined Kara, who had already introduced herself to a young couple who sat at one end of an expensive leather couch—the same couch that Drew had slept on for nearly a month.

"Let me get you both something to drink," Neil said. "What would you like, Kara?"

"How about a vodka soda?"

"My kinda girl," Neil said with delight. "How about you, bro?"

Drew hesitated. "I'm good for now, I think." *Did I really just say that?*

Neil and Kara exchanged glances, as though someone had just tried to disprove gravity.

"What do you mean?" Neil asked.

Drew wasn't sure why he had said it, but he suspected that his fleeting thought of Sierra moments before might be to blame. "I, uh, had a few earlier at dinner. Think I might wait a bit."

"I've known you three fucking years, bro, and I've never heard you say no to a drink."

"I'm trying this new thing where I make better choices."

"Better choices?"

"Yeah, getting drunk and high all the time. Life is a bunch of moments and, uh—" He tried to replicate the words of wisdom that Sierra might have offered, "—and those moments are all strung out together, or something like that. Just trying to slow down a bit, you know."

"I know you sound like a goddamn pussy at the moment." Neil howled. "That's what I know."

Not sure why I expected him to be supportive.

"Listen up, everybody." Neil raised his voice to capture the attention of the room. "Drew Thomson, the same guy who got sacked last month for snorting blow before a client meeting, is too good to have a drink at my party."

Kara offered Drew a sympathetic look as though she were affronted on his behalf.

"Was that necessary?" Drew asked with a heavy sigh.

Neil's voice returned to normal. "Listen, I know you've struggled with this shit for a while, so it's great that you're making improvements and all that. But tonight, you're at my house, at my party. You can start being a saint tomorrow. Tonight we get fucked up."

It wasn't that Neil had made a good point, it's just that Drew's self-control was already so threadbare that it took very little persuasion to pierce it. "Fine—whiskey then. I'll have a whiskey."

"Attaboy."

"Hey," Drew exclaimed before Neil could head for a bartender, "there's something else I've been meaning to tell you."

"What's that?"

"It's my dad. He's got cancer."

"Is it bad?"

"He doesn't have long left."

"Sorry to hear that." Neil inserted a somber pause, more for effect than authenticity. "Tonight we drink in his honor."

* * *

Drew couldn't decide if the music had gotten louder, or if his ability to hear his own thoughts had faded on its own. The crowd had doubled or tripled in size since he arrived and he found himself feeling claustrophobic.

He and Kara had been dancing for the last hour, her movements precise and provocative, his offbeat and inept. The DJ had transformed Neil's living space into an exclusive nightclub of sorts, activating a show of laser lights and the occasional puff of fog.

"Neil seems nice," Kara shouted over the music.

"Yeah, he's a peach, isn't he?"

"Do I detect sarcasm, Drew Thomson?"

"Not exactly."

She frowned.

Drew scanned their cups—both empty. "I'm going to get us a refill."

He walked to the nearest bartender. Staggering as his propensity for alcohol was, he found his senses dulled—the mixed drinks strong, and the straight liquor poured to the brim. But immersed in a sea of bodies as he was, his sense of unease was heightened, directing him to drink more, faster, two hands at a time if it were possible.

Neil appeared at Drew's side. "I thought you wanted to stay sober tonight."

"Looks like I don't know what I want."

* * *

Neil led a small group into his private study, ornamented with an expansive desk and numerous bookcases encompassing its perimeter. The titles in his library appeared untouched, more a display of refinement than a space for intellectual endeavors.

A number of his guests made wisecracks upon entering:

"Guess it must be story time."

"You gonna tuck us in now, Neil?"

"Since when does this guy read anything besides *Hustler*?"

I'm not even sure if Neil can read.

On the desk was a mirror, several razor blades, and a pile

of short straws. A feeding frenzy descended on the desk, like a mob at a Black Friday sale.

Between lines, Drew noticed a member of Neil's security personnel stationed at the door. Drew approached Neil, who, having not partaken himself, appeared to be supervising. "Do you really need security posted outside the door for this?"

"You can never be too careful, bro. Got to protect myself."

"How can you afford all this?"

"I told you I got promoted after you left."

"Yeah, but the condo, the furniture, the security, the booze, the drugs. Even if you doubled your salary—"

"Don't worry about it, bro."

I'm not worried. I'm confused, and more than just a little bit jealous.

With his attendees distracted, Neil pulled a small pouch of pills from his breast pocket and stashed it between two books on a nearby shelf.

"What're those?" Drew asked.

"Ecstasy, I'm told. You wanna try one?"

"Sure."

Neil raised an eyebrow. "Bro, I was kidding. These are for—"

"First you blast me for wanting to take it easy, then you won't let me have a goddamn pill?"

"Rolling on ex is one thing, but you've been drinking—a lot. And doing coke. It's gonna hit you hard."

Only if I'm lucky. "I'm a big boy, Neil. I can make my own choices." Drew swiped the pouch from the shelf and opened it, tossing two pills in his mouth, swallowing them both with greed.

"I'd better store these someplace else," Neil said, taking the pouch from Drew. "Last thing I need is you popping my entire supply like Tic Tacs."

* * *

A half hour passed and Drew felt exhilarated. He had no idea where Kara was, but he had made new friends—two of the nicest guys he had ever encountered. Drew was disoriented, uncoordinated, but somehow fluid in his interactions with others, or so he thought. His topics of conversation were riveting, his dialogue witty and charming, and his dancing electric. The DJ was playing some kind of magic music, the best songs he had ever heard.

"Bro." Neil tapped him on the shoulder. "Thought you might like to check in on Kara. She's been in the bathroom for a while now."

"But I just met these guys."

"Their names are Carl and Sanjay, and we worked with them for years. Not to mention I watched you introduce yourself to them three times already."

"No way." Drew tried to sound convincing, but his feet were floating two inches off the floor.

"Yeah, bro. Just in the last twenty minutes."

"We might have to disagree on this one."

"You're a fucking clown," Neil scoffed.

A two-man security team led a bevy of young beauties into the room, fifteen of them or more, all outfitted for merrymaking. Black, white, Asian, and Hispanic women—none of them much older than twenty-one—decorated in slinky dresses, towering stilettos, revealing skirts, and low cut tube tops.

"Is this parade of estrogen, uh, courtesy of your friend?"

Neil's face was full of anticipation. "The guy works wonders, doesn't he?"

"Your friend, what? Just goes out and, uh, invites women to parties?" Drew petted Neil while talking to him.

"He snags a few barflies, I'm sure. But being well connected is what he does best. He finds sluts who wanna party and rounds 'em up for me."

"What, like on a tour bus?" *Probably a rickety van . . .*

"I don't concern myself with details, bro."

. . . the driver baits them in the back with Louis Vuitton.

"All you need to know is these bitches are looking to go out and have a good time, so why not right here? I've got security, drinks, food, music, uppers, good people. These bitches don't care. It's all free for them. It's like going to the kind of house party you see in movies except I put on the real thing."

"And you pay this guy for his help?"

"Something like that." Neil grinned. "He usually comes to the party and gets first dibs."

"Your very own meat market, huh?" Drew snorted, becoming acutely aware of how much he appreciated his own nostrils.

"I guess, but let's be honest—none of these bitches are going to be our first woman president. Young crack whores in the making for the most part."

Drew recalled attending a number of Neil's parties over the years—there had always been a plethora of attractive women and refreshments of every variety. But even intoxicated as he was, this was the first time Drew had considered not just the cost of these parties, but their consequences. Perhaps it was because this was the most epic bash Neil had ever thrown. Like something right out of a movie, just as he had said.

The last two girls who entered with the rest caught Drew's eye. They looked conspicuously undeveloped, reserved and timid in their demeanor, unlike the others. "How old are those two?" he asked, pointing.

"How the fuck should I know?"

"Doesn't your friend, uh, check?"

"I don't tell another man how to run his business."

"They look too young to . . . " He realized he was still pointing and lowered his hand.

"You're tripping balls, bro. Settle down."

"Uh . . . "

"Let's go say hi to them."

They made their way to the two girls. The first one had freckles, braces, and pink streaks of dye in her sandy blonde hair. Her friend was about five feet tall with a fat face and a bra stuffed unevenly.

Even in his most careless moments, Drew wanted nothing to do with underage girls, although being Neil's friend felt a lot like guilt by association. But with every fleeing second, Drew had more trouble remembering why he and Neil were talking to them in the first place.

"Good evening, ladies," Neil said.

"Hi . . . " was all Freckles could manage. She seemed nervous to make eye contact with anyone in the room. She folded her arms and moved closer to her pudgy friend.

"This girl," Drew said with his lips pressed to Neil's ear, "the one with the talking freckles. She looks like she's fifteen, and her friend looks even tinier than that."

Neil rolled his eyes. "Ladies, my friend here thinks you're too young to know how to have a good time."

"We are not," Pudgy proclaimed. "We party with older guys all the time, don't we Chelsea?"

Freckles jumped in, daring herself to be heroic. "And we heard there'd be Molly at this party."

"You could learn something from these two," Neil said to Drew, turning the discussion into a teachable moment. "They know how to have a good time." He gestured down the hall. "This way, ladies. I keep a stash under my pillow." Neil pointed them in the right direction and they took off, but he lingered a moment. "You want the one in the pigtails or the chubby midget?"

"Neither. What the hell is wrong with you?"

"Your loss." Neil shrugged. "I mean, you could have them both if you want. Personally I don't fuck anything less than a nine—"

"Are we talking looks or age?"

"Very funny. Look, relax bro. I'm not gonna touch 'em. But if word gets out that there's no junk at my parties, I'll never get another busload of pussy here again. Got to give the ladies what they came for."

* * *

"Here you are! I've been looking all over for you." Kara said.

Drew was alone in the study leaned against a bookshelf, ostensibly perusing its titles, most of them in an alien language. *He's never read all these books.*

"Are you all right, Drew Thomson?" Kara approached Drew and put a hand on his shoulder. "Drew, it's me—are you feeling okay?"

Drew finally noticed her. "Oh, yeah, I'm doing good. How about you?" His speech was hollow and labored, slurred nearly beyond recognition.

"Something I ate at dinner didn't agree with me."

"What'd it say?"

"Huh? No, I mean—"

"Did you win?"

"Win what?"

"The disagreement."

Kara tittered. "Drew—"

"You said you and your dinner had a disagreement."

"Yeah, and I think the dinner won."

Drew bobbed his head. He felt the air whoosh past his ears. "Better luck next time."

"Anyway, I'm not feeling so hot. I've got a friend coming to pick me up. I'll text you tomorrow, okay?"

Drew didn't respond. He swayed in one spot, his vapid gaze burning a hole through the collection of books. *Where did all these books come from anyway?*

* * *

It was only midnight but Drew knew it was time to go.

The journey back to his car proved to be a grueling affair. His feet wouldn't move in sync at first. Then his keys went missing for a while. Once found, they wouldn't go in the ignition. The stick shift was heavier than he remembered, disinclined to budge at first. But after a few attempts and with a lot of persistence, he managed to escape from the underground parking. He began moving in the right direction, streetlights streaking his peripheral vision.

He turned on the radio to discover more magic music—just like the DJ had been playing. His car responded to the epic melodies, flying toward its destination in double time, passing other vehicles along the racetrack. He had no idea his hatchback liked to party.

Drew's phone vibrated in his pocket, electrifying his leg, as though he were having an out-of-body experience. Something was touching him . . . but by the time he realized what, it was too late to answer. "Forgot to turn off my electronics before takeoff," he said to himself with a chuckle.

He tore through the next intersection, its burning red stoplight urging him to proceed. His bald tires screeched with excitement.

Chapter 24

Lights filled his rearview mirror all at once, bouncing glowing embers off his eyes. A whole host of flashes were in pursuit, hollering, their voices like a thousand blaring sirens. He could taste his heartbeat in his throat, feel his pulse pounding.

He brought his car to a rapid halt in the middle of the lane. A powerful floodlight poured through his rear windshield from a vehicle behind him.

Drew looked up as a man in his forties approached, grim, his face worn with stress lines resembling canyons, his peppered white hair dancing in the evening breeze. "License and registration."

Drew remained motionless, racking his brain to recall what that meant. "I, uh, don't—I don't know if I have those things," he said. His hands trembled, his face was white with terror.

"You don't have a license?"

"I, uh—I probably do. But I'll be damned if I can remember where I put it."

The man twitched his nose. "Sir, have you been drinking tonight? I followed you for a while. You were all over the road."

"I might have ran a red light, too."

"Sir, I'm going to need you to step out of the car."

"Standing is hard right now," Drew whined. "I'm a bit drunk, kinda high on coke, and I just tried ecstasy for the first time—"

"Sir, step out of—"

"I should probably just take one next time." His car door flew open, as though his hatchback had decided to eject him. He set one foot on the road with pronounced difficulty, his head swimming, and struggled to pull out the other before falling out of the car.

"Can you walk, sir?"

Drew laid still, trying to remember how balance worked. "I hope so . . . let me try."

Chapter 25

Getting arrested turned out to be even less glamorous than it looked on television. Drew passed the long and restless hours in his holding cell babbling to himself, unable to sleep, incoherent and frustrated. He had mostly sobered up by sunrise, at which point he was faced with a dilemma. It was Sunday, the Fourth of July at that. The courts would be closed until Tuesday. He could sit in a cell until then, or make bail. His car had been impounded and his license suspended—a suspension he had the right to contest, but not the desire. He felt defeated.

The good news was that, unlike what he had seen on popular crime dramas, he was permitted more than one phone call. He first considered calling Logan. His legal background could prove useful. But hoping to spare himself a lecture, Drew decided against it. After getting no answer three or four times in a row, Neil finally picked up.

An hour later, Drew was escorted from his cell to collect his personal belongings—his phone, keys, and wallet—and instructed to appear at his arraignment on Tuesday. He walked outside and found Neil leaning against the building, tapping his foot, undoubtedly irritated. They walked through the parking lot to Neil's Mercedes.

"You fucking idiot," Neil said, once they were inside with the doors closed. "You got yourself arrested."

"Give it a rest, Neil. You're not the victim here. You let me wander off in the middle of the night and drive—"

"I told you not to take those pills, bro." Neil glared at him, eyes beady and bloodshot, his usual morning grooming glossed over in favor of sweat pants and a tee shirt. "That was your own stupid fucking decision." He took a moment to compose himself. "You didn't tell them where you were coming from, did you?"

"I kept you out of it."

"Thank God for small miracles . . . " He rocked his head in his hand, his arm resting against the car door. "I had to leave three fine ladies in bed this morning to come get you, you know."

If I'd have gone to prison last night, I might have ended up in bed with three fine gentlemen. "Three at once, huh? How many dicks do you have?"

"They mostly took care of each other."

Drew glanced at the dashboard. It was eight o'clock. "Look, I'm sorry, Neil. I really am. Thanks for coming to get me and thanks for bailing me out. I'll pay you back."

"Get real. You work at a fucking call center. I won't see that money again until your court date. And if you jump bail, I'll find you and fucking murder you."

"Fine. Just take me home then."

"Sure thing, bro. Some gratitude," Neil grumbled. "Where to?"

"Palmer Heights."

He laughed under his breath, his best passive aggressive attempt at condescension.

Drew scanned his phone for text messages from the night before. Its charge was nearly depleted, but it had a sliver of juice left.

Kara: *Just got home :) hope you had a fun night xoxo*

He swiped to the next conversation.

Logan: *On my way*

Logan: *Drew where are you?*

Logan: *Check your messages Drew. Call back ASAP please*

Exerting a herculean effort—his head pounding, his senses on fire—Drew raised the phone to his ear, following robotic prompts to his voicemail inbox. Four unheard messages.

"Hi Drew, it's Holly Kenney calling from Mercy Vale—it's just after midnight. I'm sorry for calling so late, but your father is having difficulty breathing. I don't want to alarm you, but if you get this message tonight, I'd recommend paying him a visit right away."

"Drew, it's Holly again. Thought I'd give you another try. I was able to get ahold of Logan—he's on his way. If you get this message, please call one of us back or get to the hospital as fast as you can. Your dad's holding on for the time being, but he might not make it through the night."

"Andrew, it's Logan. I'm at the hospital with Russell. He's choking on his own blood. They're trying to suction it, but it's not helping. You need to get down here, Andrew. Hurry."

Logan had been frantic in his first message, but in the second his sorrow was unmistakable, his voice shaky and subdued. "Where are you?" Indistinct sobs and sniffles. "He's gone, Andrew. Russell's gone."

* * *

Drew stormed into his father's room. "Dad!"

Russell's bed was empty, stripped of its sheets, the contraptions that had monitored his vitals absent. Drew stared, entombed, the morning sunlight peeking through the far window and barreling into his pupils like a freight train, his head not just throbbing, but reeling out of control. The room was noiseless, sterile, barren. It was as if his father had never been there.

"Is that you, Drew?"

But Drew heard nothing at first, deaf to the sounds of Patrick in the next bed. His ears were filled with a distant ringing noise—a high-pitched whine, as though he were suffering from shell shock. His senses were fragile, his mind unhinged.

"Drew?"

No response.

"Drew, it's Patrick—come pull back my screen."

After a moment of indecision, Drew approached the far end of the room, his feet dragging like cinderblocks and his stomach full of concrete. He retracted the privacy curtain in slow motion. There was Patrick, withered and decaying, what remained of him sitting upright in bed. "I'm sorry," Patrick said. "They wheeled your dad out in the night, and . . . " He gestured to empty side of the room, " . . . I don't think he made it."

"I wasn't here."

"What?"

"I missed the call and he died without me here."

Patrick listened, calm, allowing Drew to express his thoughts uninhibited, and then offered, "It's not your fault—you had a good reason, I'm sure. Plus your brother was here."

Drew shook his aching head. "Jail."

"Huh?"

"I spent the night in jail."

"I'm sorry it happened that way, son—"

I'm not your son.

"My wife used to have a saying." Patrick removed a photograph he had safeguarded between two pages of a Bible on his bedside table. It was a portrait of a younger version of himself alongside a heavyset woman with curly hair . . .

Coffee Breath. "I know her," Drew blurted. "This woman." He snatched the photo Patrick held out to him, tapping his finger on her face. "She was a—"

"She was a grief counselor."

"Yes, a, uh—" He was going to say Sadness Doctor. "I saw her when I was a child. I was about ten or so when Dad took me to see her."

"She worked with kids a lot of the time."

"I only met her once . . . where is she now?"

"Passed away a few years ago, my Victoria did. God rest her soul."

Drew shook, overflowing with agony and regret but astounded nonetheless, wishing he were better equipped to appreciate this discovery. "This woman changed my life."

"She'd be happy to hear that, I think. If I may ask, what did she change?"

"She changed . . . " But nothing came. "She encouraged me to keep a diary."

"Well, Vickie always had a saying. 'Live your life with purpose,' she would say, 'or life will be nothing more than passing seconds and minutes.' "

"I got arrested for drunk driving last night. I don't know that I'm living with much purpose these days."

"But you're young, Drew. Fairly young, at least. You've still got time. You can still honor your dad's memory. That's what he would have wanted."

Drew peered back at the empty bed, as if he expected to see his father there, complete with angel wings and a halo, glowing, healthy and perfect. Instead he saw nothingness— just an empty hole where Russell had endured his final days. He glanced at the photo again, and then returned it to

Patrick. "Do you still miss her?"

"It gets easier, son. Just try and focus on the special moments."

Chapter 26

It was a long cab ride back to Palmer Heights. The driver seemed bent on engaging in idle chitchat, but Drew wasn't in the mood. "I tell you, this city is going to hell fast."

"It is?"

"Yeah, we've got corrupt politicians lying through their teeth. Goddamn immigrants taking all the good jobs—"

"You seem to be doing all right."

"Yeah, buddy, I'm living the dream." He looked to be middle age, overweight, and a hint scruffier than Drew. His teeth were sparse and his words tumbled out inarticulate and muddled.

"This is my building," Drew announced. "Right up here on the left."

"Nice place," the driver commented, not a hint of mockery in his voice.

As Drew approached his apartment door, he found a document taped to it: Eviction Notice. In other circumstances, Drew might have reacted differently—tearing it down in a fit of panic or crumpling it up and tossing it away. But weary and shattered as he was, he removed it with care, unlocked his door, and went inside.

After shuffling about and trying to eat breakfast—he couldn't manage more than two bites—he dropped himself in his rocking chair, powered on his laptop, and started recording.

"I—I don't even know where to start." He kept his eyes lowered, avoiding his own reflection on the screen. "Dad's gone. Died last night, while I was at Neil's—no, while I was in jail to be more accurate. My car got impounded, I lost my license—" He glanced over at his mountain bike on the balcony. "Guess I'll be pedaling to work from now on."

Drew deliberated for a moment before getting to his feet and retrieving a sealed bottle of vodka from the kitchen. He placed it on his desk and sat down.

"I can't believe I wasn't with—" Tears fell from his face, a few at first, then a raging stream, the pent up grief of that morning spilling down his cheeks. "I just can't believe it." Regret and rage balled together in his stomach. "I never got to say goodbye . . . " Pain was unfamiliar to Drew, having spent so many years numb.

His face wet and his hands unsteady, he raised the eviction notice in full view of the camera. It looked a bit plain, like something printed on standard computer paper. "And then there's this. Rent was due on Thursday and there was nothing in my account."

One minute and eleven seconds.

His phone rang, Sierra.

Drew thought for a moment about allowing it to go to voicemail, but he recalled how that worked out the night before. He answered on the third ring. "Hello?"

"Hey Drew, it's Sierra."

"Hi."

"Is everything okay, dude?"

He contemplated for a moment. "Why wouldn't it be?"

"You texted me a photo of some books last night asking me where they came from."

"It was a long night." He sunk down further in his chair.

"Dad died just after midnight."

"Oh, wow, I'm so sorry."

The video was still recording. It seemed ironic that his webcam, attributed with chronicling special moments, was for the first time capturing life as it happened.

"Can I come see you?" she asked. "Or would you rather be left alone?"

Drew eyed the vodka in front of him. "I, uh—maybe we could get together later. I'm right in the middle of something at the moment."

"You're not drinking, are you?"

"No, I'm—I'm recording a video actually."

"Like a YouTube video?"

"More like a personal diary entry."

"You still keep a diary? I thought you said it never helped much."

Drew thought back to his conversation with Patrick that morning, the startling realization that he had been married to Coffee Breath. "I don't know. It doesn't hurt, I suppose."
Suppose, s'pose . . .

"If it helps you move forward, that's great. But if it keeps you fixated on the past, maybe it's not such a good idea."

"What do you mean?"

"I don't know. I've just always preferred the idea of creating a dream board rather than writing in a diary. Keeps me looking forward. But you must be going through hell right now. If talking it out helps, go for it. Um, Drew, can I ask you something else?"

"Yeah."

"Can you promise me you won't drink today?"

"I can't promise you that, no."

"Then can you at least wait until after I come see you?"

Drew peeked at his phone. Its battery was about to die.

"I've got to go, Sierra. I'll think about it." A knock came at the door. "I'll text you later."

"Okay. I'll be thinking about you."

"Likewise." Drew tossed his phone on the desk, curious to see what new disturbance awaited him. He opened the door.

There stood Logan, his face blotchy and somber. "Where were you?"

"I—"

"Russell died last night and you weren't there, Andrew."

"I know." Drew invited Logan inside. "I showed up this morning and it was too late."

Logan entered, pausing to embrace Drew at the door, his eyes then scanning the empty space before him. "This is where you live?" he asked, mouth agape.

"Not for long." He retrieved the eviction notice from his desk and handed it to his brother. "Any legal advice?"

Logan took it and read the first few lines. "Pay your rent on time is my best advice."

"Hysterical. I didn't get paid until Friday."

"You're living paycheck to paycheck now?"

"Jesus Christ, Logan. I asked for advice, not a sermon."

Logan exhaled deeply, plainly exasperated, and scanned the document further. "This isn't an official document, Andrew. Just something your landlord made up." He handed it back. "Plenty of slumlords do this kind of thing. It's a scare tactic. Just pay what you owe and you'll be fine."

Drew nodded. *Fucking Patel.*

"We can talk about this later, Andrew. How are you dealing with all of this?"

"I'm managing."

Logan didn't look convinced. "I've started making funeral arrangements and I'd like your input."

He didn't even want you for a son, and now you're taking care of his funeral.

"And I thought we should stop by Russell's house," Logan continued, "just to make sure everything's in order. At least until we figure out what's going to happen with his estate."

Taking a road trip with Logan didn't sound appealing, least of all now, but he had nowhere else to be. And he was duty-bound to assist, considering his brother was footing the bill. Drew closed his laptop. "I've got a spare key. Let's go."

"Your car or mine?"

"Better take yours. Mine's in the shop."

* * *

The car ride over had served as an opportunity to discuss minute details. Who would contact whom—the limited social circle Russell had—who they would ask to preside over the funeral, what type of floral arrangement would be most appropriate, and the like. In almost every case, Logan had a suggestion at the ready, to which Drew simply replied, "Sounds good."

They entered their father's house, an unopened stack of his mail in hand, and it was all the things Drew had learned to appreciate over the years—quiet, modest, and vacant. Its many riches felt like home. The old card table in front of the miniature television, the jaundiced, peeling wallpaper, and the saturation of pungent cigarette smoke in everything.

Logan walked in and marveled at its familiarity. "This place hasn't changed a bit."

Drew envisioned his father sitting at the card table—no pants, chain smoking to reruns of sitcoms, and slurping his coffee—while Logan paced between rooms, examining each one in its entirety, as though he had just stepped through a time warp. "I haven't been here in years," he said.

"How does coming back here make you feel?" Drew felt strange posing such a personal question to his brother, but unable to make sense of his own emotions, he was curious.

"I feel nothing but sadness."

"Sad that he's gone?"

"No. Well, sure, but I meant sad that he lived this way. He's at peace now, but his life was kind of tragic."

Drew was irritated at first, angry at his brother's thoughtless comment, but understood after a moment what he had meant. It *was* tragic, after all.

They spent the next hour exploring every inch of the house, uncovering old family photo albums tucked away in the basement, alongside Christmas decorations and a cigar box full of jewelery.

Logan pulled an ornamental angel out of its packaging, its left wing cracked. "Russell never could get this thing to stay on top of the tree."

Drew held up a string of pearls. "Mom used to wear these out to dinner." He examined each pearl between his fingertips. "Dad kept them all these years . . . "

They found other treasures Angela left behind: a snow globe, a handheld mirror, a silk scarf, and a short stack of handwritten notes and birthday cards. The rest of the basement was littered with shop tools, old work clothes, and a couple of bowling trophies, all coated in thick dust.

Drew flipped through the first few pages of a photo album, stopping on a black and white photo of Russell. He was handsome and muscular, his hair was neat. He stood in front of a small industrial office building, the headquarters of his once thriving business. A banner stretched above its glass doors announced its grand opening. Drew traced his father's figure, lost in thought.

They relocated to Russell's bedroom. Logan, being

slightly taller than Drew, pulled a heavy Bankers Box from the top shelf of the closet. He opened it and began sifting through its contents. Old insurance paperwork, the odd tax return, some bank statements, and then, "Andrew, did Russell have a will?"

"I have no idea. He never mentioned one. Don't think he had much to give."

"This house and his car, maybe, which we'll have to sort out, but . . . "

"Logan, take it. It's all yours as far as I'm concerned. You paid his hospital bills and, uh, I don't have much to contribute to his burial. So I think—"

Logan raised his forefinger to silence Drew. He shuffled a few pieces of paper, flipping between them. "He had a will, filed with probate court and everything."

"He did?"

Logan nodded. "Dated—wow, almost ten years ago."

"He probably forgot all about it."

"Probably." Logan read on. "His house, his car, and whatever is in his checking account—he left it all to you."

Chapter 27

They debated at length, Drew insisting that his brother take the house and sell it. He could mitigate his losses, having covered both the medical and funeral expenses. Logan declined over and over again, contending that Drew was the rightful heir to the estate.

Realizing that he couldn't persuade his brother to take it all, Drew changed his strategy, suggesting they sell their father's assets and split the proceeds down the middle. Logan still refused. "Stephen and I don't need the help," he said. "You do. Besides, you were always closer to him than I was, and he wanted you to have it. This could be your chance to start over."

Drew was maddened by Logan's stubbornness, and he resented being treated like a charity case. At the same time, he was touched by Logan's kindness. He had done nothing to earn such generosity from his brother.

In the end, Drew decided to weigh his options—to sell the house or keep it, for now. Under normal circumstances, he would have preferred the isolation of his own apartment, allowing himself to sleep on his internal conflict in his own domain. But he felt somehow apprehensive about returning to Palmer Heights for the night and elected to move into his father's house for a few days, at least until after the funeral. Perhaps to feel closer to him even after death.

Logan spent the remainder of the afternoon helping Drew relocate his belongings from his apartment to the house—everything but his thrift shop furniture and his mattress. It was a straightforward exercise, given that most of his possessions were still in boxes.

After hauling the second and final load inside—his bike had taken up most of the space on the first trip—Drew said, "There's something I've been meaning to ask you."

"What's that?"

"I've given you lots of shit for working in criminal defense."

"You have."

"What I want to know is—" He unpacked a few of his belongings, placing his laptop on the card table, along with a phone charger and his bottle of vodka, "—why choose that career path after all our family has been through?"

Logan appeared to do some soul searching. "Let me answer your question with another question. Why did you start drinking?"

"I don't know." Drew shrugged. "Wanted to numb my brain, I guess."

"You wanted to dilute your feelings, right?"

"What little feelings I actually have."

"Well, when I left home as a teenager, I started drinking, too. Then one day I said to myself, 'Why not try to understand my feelings instead of running from them?'"

"You became a lawyer to get in touch with your feelings?"

"No, but I thought it might help me understand why violent people do the things they do. Why somebody would hurt another human being the way somebody hurt Mom."

"Did it help?"

"I think so. I learned to feel compassion and I learned to let go of some of my anger." Logan scratched his head, as if debating how much he should share. "I gave up drinking before my twentieth birthday. I haven't touched the stuff since. And I've discovered that not everyone who does horrible things is a horrible person."

But you do help horrible people get away with doing horrible things . . . then again, I got charged with a crime this morning. Maybe I'm a horrible person, too.

"Doesn't make what happened to Mom right," Logan continued, "but I can't change the past. Best I can do is accept it and go on with my life and hope that karma is a real thing." Logan walked toward the door. "If you need anything, just call."

Drew found himself alone in what had always felt like his true home—his childhood home, at the very least. But even as an adult, Russell's house had come to be a safe haven of sorts. A place where he felt content to be himself, whoever that was.

Drew plugged in his phone, allowing it to charge while he took a shower. He dressed himself in one of Russell's old robes hung on the bathroom door. It smelled just like him—like cigarettes, its white cuffs stained with nicotine. He reminisced for a moment, teary, the memory of his father heavy and unrelenting. He collected himself and took a look in the fridge to discover weeks' worth of spoiled food. He pulled a can of beef stew from the cupboard and heated it on the gas stove until it was lukewarm. In the living room he turned on the small television. The size of the screen didn't matter—it was an amenity he didn't have at home. He watched a local news broadcast cover Fourth of July celebrations around town. It would be dark out soon and time for the fireworks to begin.

There was the lingering problem of the vodka in front of him. His body craved its effect, but it seemed a bit like reaching for a smoking gun. He was torn.

His phone vibrated.

Sierra: *Hey Drew. Are you ok?*

Drew: *I'm surviving*

Drew: *Sorry to cut our chat short this morning*

Drew: *Still want to get together?*

Drew: *I'm at my dad's house at the moment*

Sierra: *Family there?*

Drew: *Not anymore*

Sierra: *I can swing by if you'd like?*

Drew sent her the address and put his phone aside, battling the burning desire to drown his jumbled insides.

His guts in knots, he turned his attention to his laptop. Keeping a diary—written, visual, or otherwise—had its place. It had the potential to be an outlet for his inner workings, but in retrospect, it seemed that he most often recorded what he did for the day. His misadventures mostly. Nothing provocative or introspective, and certainly nothing that addressed the future.

Was Sierra correct that his collection of special moments was a tie to the past that he was unable to sever? Was it possible that his recorded ramblings were nothing more than an anchor to what was, an invitation to ignore what could still be? Drew thought about these things until he drifted to sleep in his father's chair, the glow of the television illuminating his face.

* * *

Rain pattered against the windows, darkness smothering the house. There was a gentle tap at the front door. Drew rose from his seat in a deliberate manner, tightening his father's robe around him. He turned on the living room lights and trotted to the door.

Sierra was soaked head to toe, clumps of wet hair matted

to her face. "Are you going to invite me in?"

He motioned for her to enter, closing the door behind her. "Did you jog over here?"

"No, I drove, but it's really starting to come down hard." She started to choke. "Oh God, dude—it smells like an ashtray in here."

"Dad was a heavy smoker, hence the lung cancer."

"Yikes. Must have been. Three packs a day I think you said."

Drew turned off the television, gesturing for her to take a seat on the couch. "Do you want anything? I, uh, don't think there's much to offer you. Soda or water, maybe."

"I'm fine." She glanced at the vodka on the table. "You been drinking?"

"No." He sat down beside her. "Haven't had a drop all day."

"How come?"

"Got myself into some trouble last night. Driving under the influence."

Sierra shook her head. "Not cool. You coulda killed someone or been killed."

"I know. Car's impounded and I lost my license for a while."

"Been a rough day, huh?"

"You have no idea."

They sat, temporarily silent, as fireworks glowed in the distance. Sierra was first to speak again. "So why your dad's place?"

"Wanted to feel close to him, I guess."

She pointed at his robe, faded and tattered. "Was that his?"

"I borrowed it for the night. Well, in fairness, this is all mine now. He left everything to me."

"Nothing for your brother?"

"No, and he's insisting he wants me to keep all of it. I think he feels sorry for me."

"Maybe he just wants to help." She looked around. "What're you going to do with it?"

"I'm going to stay here a few days and then decide."

"Think you might actually keep it?"

Drew was slow to respond. "Looks like the property taxes are paid for the year and this is the house where Logan and I grew up. Plus it's full of goodies that belonged to Mom. Maybe I could turn it into something."

Sierra took him by the hand. "I think that's the first time I've heard you talk about the future."

"So it is." *I was wondering why I had a headache.*

Sierra rested a hand on Drew's knee. "It's heartbreaking how you lost your dad. I can only imagine how much you must be hurting right now, but maybe something good can come of this." Her eyes were sincere, gifting him her undivided attention.

Drew found himself immersed in her presence, defenseless. "Can I ask you something?"

"Of course."

"Why did you kiss me in the park the other night? What was that all about?"

Sierra bit her lip. "I wanted a kiss, I guess."

"Yeah, but why?"

"Why do you think?"

He thought back to downplaying his appearance to Kara, who had promptly whacked him with her handbag. "Because I'm the best looking motherfucker in town."

She rolled her eyes.

"I'm serious. Why did you kiss me?"

"Dude, you kissed me first—on the cheek. I kissed you

back because, well, I wanted to see how it would make me feel."

"And how did it make you feel?"

"I had to go home and finger myself for hours."

"Seriously?"

"No, dude, of course not! Who do you think I am, Kara?" She cracked up. "The kiss was innocent. It felt nice, that's all. Perfect, just like it was supposed to feel."

"I actually felt connected at that moment, to another person—to you I mean. I felt connected to you at that moment."

She grinned—a goofy and toothy smile, but an honest smile—then snuggled herself against him, still damp from the rain.

"What would you do if I kissed you again?" he asked.

"I'd probably like it all over again."

He put his arm around her, drawing her to him—their lips joining to exchange an embrace that stopped time, a kiss that had the warmth to melt ice. Their lips parted after a moment, both of them reluctant, their eyes still shut tight.

"Come here," she said at last. She guided Drew's head to her chest where she held it for a minute—her heartbeat in his ear—then moving it to her lap, running her fingers through his hair, reassuring him back to sleep, the lullaby of the evening rainfall cleansing the day's events.

Chapter 28

The morning sun spilled into the living room. Drew was spread out on the couch, alone, his arms folded across his chest. It appeared Sierra had let herself out.

Slowly, deliberately, he crossed to the card table, glaring at the vodka. He took the bottle in his hand for a beat, his fingers clasped to its sealed cap. He twisted it open and moved to the kitchen, pouring the contents of the bottle in the sink. He lingered for a moment, staring into the stainless steel drain, watching the final splashes of vodka tumble to their death. A sense of panic washed over him, followed by a calming sense of relief.

He changed out of his father's robe, grabbed his bike, and walked out the door.

* * *

Drew sucked in the crisp morning air, the long bike ride to Transtel having winded him. Short hills felt like mountains, his aching legs rebelling against the workout.

Yesterday had been the Fourth of July, making today a federal holiday, but not for Transtel employees. Drew was scheduled to start work in twenty minutes. He ventured to the secluded cubicle on the far side of the call center floor and rounded its corner.

"You're here early," Hungry Paul remarked.

"I wanted to talk to you."

He minimized a few reports on his screen, then swiveled his chair to face Drew. "Please, sit."

"No, it's okay, Paul. I won't be long. Dad died on the weekend."

"Oh, Drew, I'm—"

You're sorry, right? You and everybody else. "No, let me finish. I came by to tell you that I won't be coming back."

"You're entitled to three days of bereavement."

"*Ever*, is what I was going to say, Paul. I won't be coming back ever."

Hungry Paul feigned surprise. It likely wasn't his first time having someone quit the call center on the spot. "Are you sure?"

"Yeah, I am. I spent the weekend giving it some thought. This isn't the place for me."

"Well, I'm sorry to hear that, Drew." He returned to his computer screen, reopening the reports he had been reviewing. "You'll be missed."

* * *

Drew felt nostalgic. He slowed his pedaling, giving his creaking chain a rest, noting familiar landmarks. His favorite spot for burgers, a small arcade, and, of course, the liquor store. *It's a wonder they didn't go out of business after I moved.* The dull ache of withdrawal wore at him, grating his senses. He knew a drink would fix it, but only for so long.

He left his bike in the building lobby, fairly certain no one would steal it. A beaten up bike came with built-in insurance, he reasoned—thieves weren't likely to snatch it.

He knocked on his old door and it swung open moments later.

"Hi, Heather."

"I've been worried about you. Do you want to come in?" She held the door open wide.

Drew scanned his former living space from the threshold. It reminded him of a distant dream. Heather had moved a few things around, but it was mostly unchanged. "No, I'm fine right here, thanks, and I'm sorry to come by without warning."

"Is everything okay?"

"Dad's gone."

"Oh, I'm so sorry," she said, reaching for him. "How are you coping?"

"I'm, uh, turning a new leaf, I guess."

Heather gave him a timid smile, as though his response wasn't what she had anticipated. She likely suspected he would be blackout drunk at this point, gambling away whatever money he didn't have. But here he was on Monday morning, sober as a priest, eager for confessional.

"I'm, uh—I'm taking this as a sign, I guess," Drew said. "That it's time to get my life back on track."

"Do you want to talk about it?"

"Actually, I came over because I owe you an apology."

She stared at him in silence, her expression urging him to proceed.

"I meant what I said—you deserve better. You really do. The truth, Heather, was that I never really loved you—"

"Drew—"

"I'm not saying I led you on, at least not on purpose. I just didn't know any better. I always wanted to love you. I cared for you the best I knew how. But when it came down to it, I wasn't being fair to you. That's why I left."

She nodded, surges of disappointment and acceptance alternating on her face.

"I guess I wasn't ready to admit that until now."

"I understand."

"I know you do. And I'm so sorry for all the hurt I

caused. But losing Dad showed me that it isn't too late. I don't have to live my life the way he lived his. I can . . . " He faltered, giving his mind a chance to consider what he was about to say. "I can live my truth before it's too late."

* * *

Drew entered his apartment Monday afternoon. With the boxes gone, it looked even more hollow than before.

He'd stopped for lunch on the way over, hoping food might distract him from the pangs of withdrawal he felt. His mind taunted him without mercy, urging him to give in, reminding him that one more drink wouldn't make a difference. It felt good in a strange sort of way. It was a reminder that he was winning.

Tucked into one corner beneath the kitchen sink were two small baggies—his remaining supply of weed and coke. Drew had hid them when Logan was helping him move. He placed them on his desk and pulled out his phone.

Marcus answered. "Drew! Long time, man."

"Just a few days, really."

"Right. So what can I get for you?"

"Can you come by my apartment?"

"Sure thing. Gimme five."

The call ended and a text message came in.

Kara: *Paul said you quit???*

Drew: *I did.*

Kara: *WHY??*

Drew: *I'll fill you in later*

Kara: *You always do ;)*

Drew: *Dad's funeral is Thursday at 10. Hillcrest cemetery*

Kara: *I'll ask Paul for the day off*

A knock at the door.

Drew let Marcus in, who instantly noted the missing boxes. "Are you moving again?"

"Something like that."

"Damn. I hate to lose a customer." He snapped his fingers. "Hey, you still owe me money. Can I get that from you?"

Drew passed the two baggies to Marcus. "Will this cover it?"

Marcus took a baggie in each hand, lifting them one at a time, as though he were a human digital scale. "Close enough, although I don't usually accept returns." He stuffed the product in his pocket. "Hey, how come you don't want this stuff anymore? Did you find Jesus or something?"

"Not exactly. Just, uh, hoping for a clean start."

Marcus bobbed his head in agreement, but his face said he wasn't sure what that meant. "All right, well, it's been a pleasure doing business with you."

"Likewise."

* * *

Drew knocked on the door. A placard below its peephole read, Superintendent. Mr. Patel opened up, wrinkling his face once he recognized his guest. "What can I do for you, Mr. Thomson?"

He withdrew the bogus eviction notice from his pocket, crumpled it, and tossed it to Patel, hitting him in the neck. "The place is all yours."

"But Mr. Thomson," Patel scrambled to pick up the paper ball, "you haven't given a proper notice."

"Thought you wanted me gone?"

"I want you to pay your rent on time, Mr. Thomson."

"You've got my security deposit. Keep it. Plus I left you a desk and a mattress. They're all yours—"

"You can't just walk out on your lease."

"I can and I will." He handed Patel the keys to his apartment. "Here you go."

210

"There will be legal consequences for this—"

"I bet. Sue me. Have a nice day."

* * *

Drew's ride to Hillcrest Cemetery had been his slowest of the day. He was exhausted, but more than anything, he felt uneasy. He'd always been drawn to his mother's memory, but more than ever at this moment.

He stood at her grave, his bike resting against a nearby tree.

"I guess Dad will be joining you soon—or maybe he already has. I'm a bit unclear on how it all works. I mean, he's gone, but we haven't buried him yet."

Her headstone, the one grave marker for both of his parents, would soon need to be updated to include the date of his father's death. He had died early on the Fourth of July, but Drew wondered if his date of death ought to mirror his mother's, the fifteenth of June. *It was the day he stopped living, after all.*

"When you died it changed all of us. It's only now I can see that clearly. It left Logan with something to prove. It held Dad in place. And it left me . . . " He choked for a moment, tears pooling under his eyes. "It left me hollow and trying to fill the void however I could."

This wasn't dissimilar to talking to his webcam—he was alone, narrating a special moment never to be heard or seen again. But in the presence of his mother, Drew found himself being honest in a way he never could with himself.

"You were one powerful woman, Mom. Your life and death affected us all." He lowered his voice to a faint whisper. "Take good care of Dad, okay? He's waited his whole life to be with you again."

Chapter 29

His arraignment was swift and painless. It took hours for Drew to get in front of a judge, but once he did, it was over in a matter of minutes.

Indicating that he did not have representation, the judge appointed an attorney to him then and there. The attorney—a public defender of sorts, Drew surmised—coached him to enter a plea of not guilty.

"But I am guilty."

"Listen buddy, everyone in this courthouse is guilty. I know it and the judge knows it, too. But it's my job to make sure you get a fair trial."

"I'm not sure I deserve a fair trial."

"Look, you posted bail—you obviously want to be a free man. And you have the right to stand on your innocence."

What innocence?

"If you tell the judge you're guilty, it's over. Plead not guilty and your trial probably won't be for a few weeks. My best advice? Hire the best lawyer you can afford before then."

Drew did as he was told. The judge accepted his plea, and imposed a condition on his release—to abstain from drugs and alcohol until his trial.

Chapter 30

It was Wednesday evening and well after sunset. Visitation hours had ended at the funeral home, less than ten mourners having passed through to pay their respects.

Drew and Sierra were completing another lap around Northwood Park. Neither one had been keeping track but it seemed to Drew they had circled his mother's bench at least five times. "Found out today I'm now a size thirty-eight waist," he said, almost bragging.

"Get out of here."

"It's true. Guess I put on a few pounds. Had to get a rush job done on my suit pants. Got them taken out just before my arraignment yesterday."

"And after all this walking we've been doing." She turned her head toward him. "Figure out what you're going to do with your dad's place?"

"I'm gonna keep it," he replied. "I'll get to work later this week, start clearing it out and making it my own. It'll probably take me a while."

"How are you going to support yourself?"

"The place is paid for, and there's a few antiques I can sell."

"You don't want to keep some of that stuff?"

"Some of it. A few keepsakes, but the rest can go. Already hauled one load down to the pawnshop last night. Plus I've got my hatchback listed on Craigslist. Dad's Buick is an antique itself, but it's got low miles on it and it's in good shape. When I get my license back, I can drive that. In the meantime, I really only have to keep myself fed. He had a few bucks in his checking account. Not a fortune, mind you, but enough for me to survive for a while."

"Have you told your brother yet?"

"That I'm keeping the house?"

"Yeah."

Drew shrugged. "I mentioned it today. I still have no idea why he's letting me have it. It's as much his as it is mine."

"Maybe he's doing it because he loves you."

"I doubt that."

"How come?"

"I'm, uh, a bit unlovable."

Sierra gave Drew a shove. "I wouldn't say that."

Drew stopped and faced her, her bottomless blue eyes lighting up the night sky. "You get to meet Heather tomorrow, by the way—my ex."

"Oh yeah? Think I should I have some fun with her?"

"It's Dad's funeral. I mean, probably not." Drew wasn't even sure why he was protesting. She was clearly kidding and probably just hoped to make him smile.

Sierra did her best impression of a cheerleader type—a bottled blonde, ditzy and slutty—embarking on an imaginary conversation with Heather. "Ooh, does he like his women shaved, Heather?" she asked, twirling her hair around her finger.

"Stop it." Drew failed to mask his amusement.

"Tell me, Heather, does he like having his woman on top?" She burst out in laughter, Drew following her lead, weaving his fingers between hers. Her voice returned to normal. "It doesn't bother me, dude. She's in the past."

Chapter 31

It was a simple funeral. A nondenominational minister conducted the service, reading the odd passage of scripture—none of it uplifting—and leading the group in somber prayer.

I'll bet Father Doom 'n Gloom does this same damn routine every week.

The ground had been unearthed next to his mother, his father's ornate casket hoisted above its depths. Drew, Sierra, Logan, Stephen, and Heather were gathered at its edges, joined by a ragtag trio of casual acquaintances—one of Russell's former coworkers and two of his bowling teammates. Kara was absent, having not extended so much as a call or a text since Monday. Not that Drew minded. She could be classy, charming, and certainly pleasing to look at, but he decided it was just as well that her and Sierra weren't occupying the same space. He had notified Neil of the funeral arrangements earlier that week, but received no response. His father had never met Neil in life, and it appeared they would remain strangers in death.

The funeral came to a close, the casket lowered into the ground, the final chapter written on Russell's grim legacy. Logan dropped a handful of dirt into his fresh grave. Drew wanted to do the same, but he was four days sober and preferred not to draw attention to his shaking hands.

There was a part of Drew that was convinced he was burying a version of himself—the one that thrived on complacency, dependence, and self-loathing. But not the man he was becoming. That man was budding with drive, conscience, and empathy—fibers of his character emerging for the first time.

Sierra touched his arm. "You were brave."

"I was ready."

Drew stared into the blackness below for several minutes, the other mourners relocating, granting him ample space, assembling at the bottom of the hill—the same spot where he, Logan, and Russell had parked to visit Angela a month before. He closed his eyes.

Mom took a piece of us all when she died, I think. But it's only now I realize the gift she left behind. She gave us an opportunity to do right by her. To live and love and laugh in her honor. Her memory should have brought out the best in us, not the worst. A piece of me died with you, too, Dad, but you've given me so much hope . . . so much to live for. I wish it hadn't taken so long to figure this all out. I'll do my best to make you proud. He smirked. *And, uh, I'm sorry in advance if you hate what I end up doing with your place. Haunt me if you must, but just know that I'll be all right.*

"Andrew," Logan called for him. He was swapping hugs and handshakes with the few who had been present, including Father Doom 'n Gloom.

I guess this is it. Goodbye, Dad.

Drew ambled down the hill. He shook hands with the minister, the three acquaintances, and Heather. He gave her a sincere embrace. "Thanks for being here. It meant the world to me."

"Your dad meant a lot to me, too." She glanced over Drew's shoulder in Sierra's direction, who was chatting with Stephen, allowing the two brothers all the time they needed.

"She seems nice."

"I, uh, listen, Heather—"

"I don't need any explanations, Drew. I meant what I said—she seems nice. And I really do hope you find happiness." She got in her car.

Logan approached. "It all happened so fast," he said. "Can't believe Russell's really gone."

"Me neither."

"Listen, Andrew, I was hoping you and Sierra might join Stephen and I for lunch. I know you haven't had much of a chance to get to know each other."

"I'd love to. I really would."

"But?"

"But there's something else on my mind. I promise, though. You have my word. We'll all get together soon."

Chapter 32

Darkness was descending as Drew arrived on two wheels to see Neil. After a short chat with security, he boarded the elevator and sped upward.

Neil answered the door after a short delay, shirtless, his expression cold. "What do you want?"

"Dad's funeral was this morning."

"That's why you're at my door? Because I missed your old man's funeral?"

"Actually, I wanted to apologize for how I acted at your party and thank you for bailing me out."

Neil looked down. "Whatever, bro. It's all good."

"Is that really why you weren't there? You're pissed because I asked you to bail me out?"

"You want to know why I'm pissed?" he asked, clenching his jaw. "I'm pissed because I was good to you, bro. Brought you into my home when you had no place to go. Got you coke when you were too dumb to find it on your own. Introduced you to good people, even though you always make a jackass of yourself. You should get tested for Asperger's, you fucking retard. Then you land yourself in jail and call me to make it all go away. A real man handles his own shit, bro. Grow a fucking pair. You're a waste. Just a sloppy fucking waste."

A young woman's voice echoed behind Neil. "Come back

to bed, Neil Galloway."

That voice . . . Drew's eyes widened. "Is that Kara?"

"So what if it is?"

"I bring her to one party and you pounce on her like it's open season."

Her voice again. "I'll let you stick it anywhere you'd like." She teased Neil in a singsong tone. "Don't make me beg for it again."

"Some best friend *you* are," Drew scoffed.

"I'm not your friend, bro, and she's not your girlfriend either. Just another bitch in need of a good fuck. Get over it."

"I have somewhere to be."

"Don't let the door hit you in the ass," Neil hollered after him. "Enjoy your life in Palmer Heights."

* * *

Crickets chirped in the yard, the night sky clear, vast and black, penetrated only by the pastel glow of the constellations. Their distant sparkle peered through the bedroom window, dancing, twinkling, igniting the pale walls.

Sierra had insisted that if she were going to stay the night, something had to be done about the bed sheets—saturated as they were with the odious stench of cigarettes. Searching the linen closet, Drew had found a silk set—seemingly unused, but in dire need of a wash.

Once the bedding was sorted, they had turned in for the night, succumbing to their urges, their flesh eager to intertwine—passionate, feverish, and intense, but loving, genuine, and vulnerable in equal measure. The fresh bedding added a shield of coolness afterward, its smooth tactility soothing to their ravaged bodies.

Sierra laid on her side, Drew nestled in behind her, his arm wrapped around her soft breasts. "What a day," he said.

He wasn't prone to such contrived expressions, but it seemed fitting. It had been a day wrought with grief, but a day of enlightenment, too. He had shed his excess baggage, discarded the chains that had held him in place.

Sierra kissed his hand, her body tight against his, her warmth calming to his soul. "I'm proud of you." She snickered all of sudden, as if something funny had just popped in her head. "But dude, seriously. Kara was there?"

"Yup."

"What a dirty whore."

Drew kissed the back of her neck, his lips traveling to her shoulder blade. "I thought you said you don't judge other people's sexual exploits."

"Not unless they involve you."

"Uh oh," Drew teased. "Sounds like someone is getting possessive."

She rolled on her back and met his spirited gaze, a pretend look of offense on her face, and stuck out her tongue. They both erupted in emphatic glee. He kissed her slow and deep. "Don't worry about Kara—"

"Dude, I'm not worried. I just think she's twisted, that's all."

Drew held still for a moment, allowing himself to be overcome by an unfamiliar sensation. "I think I'm—" He hesitated. "I think I'm happy, Sierra, and I know it sounds selfish, but that's all that matters. I think I'm actually happy for once. And that's saying a lot."

Chapter 33

Drew dipped his roller in the tray, sopping up fresh paint. Mushroom, the color was called, although Drew thought of it simply as off-white. "Almost done," he said.

Sierra wiped her brow. "Good." She was focused on the trim around the windows, a job that Drew detested. "I'm getting hungry."

Weeks of sweltering summer had passed, and Drew worked tirelessly on his father's house—now his house, to be more accurate. It was a labor of love and it was all he could think of, aside from Sierra, who occupied the rest of his consciousness.

"Oh, I almost forgot. My brother and Stephen are coming over for dinner tonight."

"You talked to your brother today?"

"I did."

"And?"

Drew set the roller in the tray, turning to face Sierra. "He agreed to represent me in court."

Sierra let her brush drop to the living room floor, splattering paint on clear plastic sheets. She clapped her hands. "I knew he'd help you!"

Drew let out a deep breath. "Didn't make asking him any easier." He approached Sierra, pulling her close, bringing his lips to hers. "Thanks for all your support."

"Are you sucking up so I'll cook dinner again?"

"More root vegetables? I'll pass."

"Dude, you can't cook to save your life. What are you gonna make us? Toast?"

"I have something else in mind," he said, leading Sierra to the kitchen. "Come check this out." His laptop was sitting on the counter.

"New video diary?"

"Nope."

Drew had sat in front of his laptop for almost an hour that morning, attempting to record a new entry. But the words came out clumsy and forced.

"I deleted them all, believe it or not. Every last one."

"Oh?"

"Not trying to erase the past or anything. Just content to look forward for a change." He pulled up a browser window—a tutorial on grilling. "This is what I wanted to show you."

She scanned the screen. "I didn't even know you had a grill."

"It's a bucket of rust, but it'll do for now."

They walked back to the living room. He hesitated to get back to work, his eyes lingering on a stack of picture frames he'd pulled from the walls.

Sierra followed his line of sight. "What's on your mind?"

"Have you ever thought about getting married?"

"Are you crazy?"

"I didn't mean us. Not today at least. I just mean, you know, in general."

"It's such an outdated concept, for starters. The ring, the dress no one ever wears again—"

"A city hall wedding then."

"Listen, dude. Marriage isn't a prescription for happiness

the way people think it is. There are tons of unhappy married people."

"What about my brother and Stephen? They seem happy."

"They do, but it isn't because they're married. It's because they're in a loving relationship." She gave her head a shake. "You know how I can spot the married couples in restaurants?"

"How?"

"They're the ones not talking to each other." She touched his arm. "I love that you're thinking about the future, I really do. But marriage is just one of those things people usually do for all the wrong reasons."

"I guess." Drew picked up his parents' wedding photo. "They just look so happy."

"They probably were," she said, giving the photo a hard look. "Your mom was beautiful."

"She still is."

"Do you believe that? That your mom is still with you somehow?" She asked without a hint of judgment in her voice.

Drew was slow to respond, giving himself a chance to consider her question. *I always wished Mom could guide me from beyond the grave.* He couldn't recall if he'd ever shared that thought with Sierra. "I'll never know for sure." He placed the frame back on the stack. "I guess all that matters is that everything worked out all right."